C000083928

NEXT DOOR MIDLIFE BEAR

FATED OVER FORTY

MEG RIPLEY

SHIFTER NATION

Copyright © 2022 by Meg Ripley
www.authormegripley.com

All rights reserved. Printed in the United States of America. No part of this book may be used or reproduced in any manner whatsoever without written permission except in the case of brief quotations embodied in critical articles or reviews.

This book is a work of fiction. Names, characters, businesses, organizations, places, events and incidents either are the product of the author's imagination or are used fictitiously. Any resemblance to actual persons, living or dead, events, or locales is entirely coincidental.

Disclaimer

This book is intended for readers age 18 and over. It contains mature situations and language that may be objectionable to some readers.

CONTENTS

NEXT DOOR MIDLIFE BEAR

NEXT DOOR MIDLIFE BEAR

FATED OVER FORTY

1

"REMIND ME AGAIN WHY WE DIDN'T HIRE MOVERS."
Tricia Fitzpatrick put yet another box on top of one
of the numerous stacks already littering the living
room. Well, it was supposed to be the living room.
Right now, it was just a cardboard jungle gym.

"Because we're strong and independent," her
twin sister Tara reminded her. "Or some crap like
that."

Shaking out her arms, Tricia reached up to read-
just her ponytail. "I guess I thought all this physical
labor would be a cakewalk after being on my feet
every day in the salon."

"Doing highlights isn't exactly the same as
hefting boxes and furniture all day," Tara pointed

out. She put her hands on her hips and looked around. "This is a pretty great place, you know."

Tricia frowned at the ancient crown molding, the wobbly hardwood floors, and the odd layout. She could see the kitchen through the doorway, where someone had attempted to make the old room look bright and fun with a coat of sunshine-yellow paint. It hadn't worked, and it definitely didn't hide the discolored linoleum floor. "You're just saying that because you weren't the one who inherited it."

"I've got my hands plenty full with this whole winery thing. Cloud Ridge is beautiful, but I don't have a clue how to run it, and there's a ton of pressure on my shoulders, considering the place has been winning awards." Tara crossed the room to examine the windows on the front of the house.

"Way to make me feel better about it," Tricia remarked. "Do you hear music?"

Tara paused and listened, but she shook her head. "Nope. Probably just ghosts."

"Sure, why not add ghosts to the list of shit I have to deal with? There are probably bats in the attic and giant spiders in the bedroom, just waiting to land on me when I fall asleep. Honest to god, I think this was Fiona's last prank on me. She knew I hated getting my hands dirty, so she left me her rundown farmhouse and a friggin' pumpkin patch. Shoot me now."

Tara smiled brightly. "Hey, you've been complaining about being tired of all the busybody gossip and long hours at the salon. All this fresh country air and a beautiful old house with a ton of history could be a great change for you. Remember looking through this weird window when we were kids? The glass is all wavy. It's probably from the late eighteen hundreds when this place was built."

"You don't say," Tricia frowned at her sister. "My life's dream is now complete."

"You never did appreciate history. Do you mind if I run upstairs? I want to see if Fiona left any antiques in the bedrooms." Tara pointed toward the stairs.

"Have at it, but watch out for those ghosts. I hear they like to possess women who tease their little sisters."

Tara was already halfway up the stairs. "You're only two minutes younger than me!"

"And you're two minutes older, you hag! You'll fit right in with the ghosts." Tricia smiled as she turned back toward the boxes. She and Tara hadn't been able to spend much time together over the last few years. She'd been too busy doing hair, and Tara had been swept up in her helicopter-mom duties. It was good to have her there.

Tricia turned her focus back to getting the place organized. At forty-four, she hadn't planned to pick up and move her whole life. Not until the farmhouse had been left to her, along with what seemed like the perfect opportunity to hit the refresh button on life. She'd come up there hoping it would be even better than a new hair color or a good blowout, but so far, it was just a lot of sweat and work. And creepy ass cobwebs.

It didn't help that she wasn't used to living in the country. Hardly anyone was out there, and though that sounded peaceful right now, it would probably be pretty lonely in the winter.

The music she thought she'd heard earlier started up again. No, not music, exactly. Singing. A male baritone, smooth and steady as it belted out some tune she didn't know.

Tricia walked slowly through the living room, wondering if Tara really had managed to find some ghosts upstairs, but the sound got quieter. She moved back the other way, closer to the kitchen doorway. Nothing was happening in the kitchen, and no radios had been left on.

Stepping back into the living room, Tricia

grabbed the cord for the blinds and yanked them up. The first thing she saw was the thick layer of dust that would need to be cleaned off sooner rather than later.

The second thing she saw was that she definitely wasn't alone.

The houses out there were few and far between, but the nearest neighbor was close enough that she could see straight into the window. The curtains had been drawn back, revealing a buck-naked man stepping out of the shower. Tricia knew she should look away. It was a total invasion of his privacy, whoever he was, but her eyes were glued to the scene before her. The man continued to sing as he grabbed a crisp white towel and dried off his hair, moving down to attend to his muscular shoulders and attractive arms.

He paid attention to his chest next, and so did Tricia. She leaned against the sill, wondering how a man could look that perfect. "Bet he doesn't have an ass," she murmured.

As though he'd heard her, the man turned around to grab something off the counter and proved her completely wrong. As he toweled off his upper back, his firm, sculpted cheeks were on full display.

"What's up?" Tara asked as she thundered down the stairs and jumped off the last two.

"Nothing!" Tricia snagged the cord and sent the blinds clattering back down to the sill. "Just... checking out the pumpkins."

"I wish I knew how to help you, but I guess we both have a lot to learn." Tara grabbed her purse from on top of the nearest stack of boxes. "I just realized I'm running late for my meeting with the winery manager. I'm so sorry, but I can come back and help you unpack later."

"It's fine. Don't worry about it. You've got a lot to do at your place, too. We'll get together later." She grabbed the nearest box and lifted the flaps open, needing to find some way to move and burn off all her nervous energy. Tricia waited until her sister was out the front door before she turned around and yanked the blinds open again, sending a whirl of dust into the air. The bathroom window just on the other side of the narrow strip of pumpkin field was now dark, and the naked man wasn't there anymore.

Disappointed, but knowing this would at least keep her on track with what she was supposed to be doing, Tricia turned to the box she'd opened. Several items were wrapped in tissue, and she smiled as she lifted out the one on top: a stained glass sun catcher in the shape of a sunflower, a gift from Fiona over two decades ago. Her aunt had said it reminded her of Tricia's bright blonde hair, and Tricia had kept it hanging up ever since. Cleaning off the dust from the glass, she put it up in the window she'd just been looking out of.

The knock on the door made her jump before she could pull the next thing out of the box. Tricia frowned, wondering if Tara had forgotten something. Her twin would've let herself in, though, and Tricia didn't know anyone else in Carlton. She crossed the room and opened the creaky old door.

She had to stop her mouth from falling open. Tricia had seen the man standing on her porch before. Just not with his clothes on.

She could tell now that his hair wasn't as dark as it'd looked when he'd just stepped out of the shower. It was more of a soft brown, contrasting nicely with his dark blue eyes. He'd covered up that delicious body with a t-shirt and jeans, but that didn't stop her from appreciating what she knew was underneath.

He held out his hand. "Hi. I'm your neighbor, Chief McMillan."

"Chief?" she stuttered as she reached out to take his hand, wondering if he could feel the same zing up his arm that she did when their fingers touched.

"Yes. I'm the chief of police here in Carlton."

Of course he was. She'd inherited a weird old pumpkin patch with a house that might as well be haunted, and she'd already spied on the chief of police on her first day in town.

"I see. And did you come here to arrest me for being a peeping tom?"

Still holding onto her hand, he leaned toward her slightly as he raised an eyebrow. "Should I be?"

Her lips quivered as she tried not to laugh. "At the very least, you should get some curtains for your bathroom window. You gave me quite the show this morning. I guess that's one way to welcome someone to the neighborhood." Not that Tricia minded in the least. He was damn handsome, and now that he was standing right there in her doorway, he was just as sexy. His simple pocket tee draped nicely around his muscular form, and apparently, he was one of the few guys on the planet who actually knew how to buy jeans that fit.

Chief McMillan finally let go of her hands and put his thumbs in his pockets. He grimaced as he rocked back on his heels. "Sorry about that. No one's been living here for quite some time, and I got used to doing my own thing without too much worry. I'll be sure to run to the store today."

Tricia could hardly believe she'd even told him what she'd witnessed, but it was already out there in the air where she couldn't do anything about it. She pushed the creaky door open wider. "Hey, don't change your life on account of me. Would you like to come in? Not that there's much to see. I'd offer you something to drink, but I haven't even been to the grocery store yet."

"Don't worry about that." He strode into the maze of cardboard boxes, and when he looked around the room, she thought she saw appreciation on his face instead of pure disdain at the mess. His eyes traced along the mantel and the banister instead of the piles of her belongings. "This is a great old place. I'd been wondering what would happen to it now that Mrs. Johnston had passed away. I don't think I ever saw a for sale sign, although no one would've noticed it out here, anyway."

"That's because it wasn't for sale," Tricia explained. She left the big door open so that the clean autumn breeze could come through the screen door. Maybe it would blow some of this dust away. "Fiona Johnston was my aunt, and I inherited the place."

"Oh." He stopped staring at the medallion above

the light fixture and looked down at her, his gaze intense. "I'm so sorry for your loss."

Another thrill of excitement shot through her, the kind she'd never found when she'd agreed to a dinner or two from one of those online dating sites. This guy had some serious animal magnetism, for sure. "Thank you. She was a great lady, but she also had a great sense of humor. I'm pretty sure that's why she left me this place. She's laughing in her grave right now, knowing I'm living in the middle of a field of pumpkins that I don't know jack about."

Chief McMillan smiled. "I met her a few times, and I think you just might be right. So what are you going to do with these pumpkins, then?"

Tricia moved to the front window. The pumpkin fields were mostly all around the back-side of the house, stretching across the strip of land that lay between her place and Chief McMillan's bathroom window, and then edging right up to the front lawn. The long vines crawled across the ground, with bright orbs of color hanging off of them here and there. She spotted something that didn't quite look like it was the right shape. Was that even a pumpkin? Or had Fiona left her even more surprises? "I don't have a clue. I'll have to do some research, I guess, since I'm already surrounded by them. Oh, hell. Can I even get online way out here?"

He chuckled softly. "We're not completely in the boondocks. It might take the company a while to get to you, but they'll do it. Listen, I've got to get going, but is there anything you need a hand with?" Chief McMillan spread his large hands to indicate the surrounding mess.

Tricia bit her bottom lip. How tempting would it be to have him help her with these boxes or move the couch under the window where she wanted it? She'd get to see that hot body at work, although she was pretty sure she'd be the one getting sweaty.

She shook her head, though, remembering this was reality and not some fantasy. "No, that's okay. I got everything off the truck, and I still have to figure out where to put everything."

"All right. Well, if you need anything, I'm right next door." He pointed with his thumb toward the exact window she'd initially seen him through.

"You certainly are," she said with a smile as she opened the screen door. "It was nice to meet you, Chief."

"Please, call me Duke." With one last gorgeous smile, he was out on the porch.

Tricia let the screen door close, then shut the

front door and leaned against it. "Lusting after my new neighbor? Am I really that hard up?" she asked herself.

Apparently, the answer was yes, because a moment later, she shot across the living room. Dodging around a box of towels, she peeked through the blinds to see Duke cutting through the pumpkin patch. His long strides carried him quickly back to his place, and she noted that his ass still looked damn good in those jeans.

Stepping back before there was any chance of him seeing her, Tricia cranked up some music. She had to get to work, not only because she had no idea where most of her clothes and dishes were. She needed to work off all this energy she suddenly had inside her.

2

"Why are we having oatmeal?"

"Because it's good for you."

"I don't care. I don't like it. It's old people food."

"*I* like oatmeal. Are you saying I'm old?"

"Well, I... I mean... That's not what I meant."

Duke smiled at the conversation as he walked in the front door. He didn't have to be in the kitchen to know that Oliver was the one protesting his breakfast. At nine years old, he was getting to the age where he questioned authority. Even having the chief of police as his father didn't change that. Having Emily around just might. He stepped into the kitchen to see that all three of his children were up, dressed, and eating breakfast.

Mia was leaning forward, digging her spoon into

the bottom of her bowl. "I like the peaches in the oatmeal."

"But you have to eat more than just the peaches," Emily reminded her.

"Hi, Dad!" Mason cried out when he saw him come in. He scooped up a big spoonful of oatmeal, ready to show that *he* wasn't the one arguing with the nanny. "Where did you go?"

"Just next door." Duke crossed the kitchen to the coffeepot, thrilled to see that it was freshly brewed and still piping hot. He'd brought Emily on to take care of the children, but she had a way of taking care of him, too. "We have a new neighbor."

"Who is it?" Oliver asked, still frowning at his oatmeal. "Are there kids over there to play with?"

"I'm afraid not, buddy." At least, Tricia hadn't mentioned any children. He hadn't even bothered to ask. Duke had been too busy staring at her house to make sure he wasn't staring at her. "It's just a lady named Tricia."

"I like that name," Mia said around a mouthful of peaches. "Is she pretty?"

"Don't talk with your mouth full," Emily chided. "Duke, there's plenty more oatmeal in the pot."

Duke occupied himself with grabbing a bowl and dishing up a hearty serving while he thought about that. Was Tricia pretty? Pretty didn't even begin to describe her. As soon as she'd opened that door, his entire body had reacted to her, all the way down to the soul of his bear. Those sweet brown eyes, her blonde hair thrown up into a messy ponytail, and even the way her faded R.E.M. t-shirt clung to her had driven him wild. Holy hell. He might not have asked if there were children, but did she have a husband? "Yes, she's pretty," he replied mildly.

"So, someone's finally taking over the pumpkin patch?" Emily asked as she ran a rag under the faucet and wiped down the counter.

"She's not sure what she's doing with it yet." And Duke wasn't sure what to do with himself. He'd made his excuses and left her house quickly enough, but he longed to go back. His bear was almost demanding it of him, which was strange. Tricia was human, as far as he could tell. Regardless, he shouldn't have feelings like that for someone. Not now, and maybe not ever. He wanted to mull over his thoughts, but as a forty-five-year-old single dad and police chief, his life was too full to afford much time to just sit and think.

Mason was carving pictures into the surface of his oatmeal with the edge of his spoon. "Can we go meet her?"

Duke sat down at the table across from the twins and focused on his meal. Kids were going to ask questions. They always did, and he was more than happy to answer most of them. He'd only just met Tricia, but she was already proving to be a difficult subject. "Sometime. Right now, we need to let her get settled in. Everything's still in boxes over there."

Oliver fished a peach slice out of his oatmeal and let it fall back into the bowl with a plop. "Dad, I found the Halloween costume I want, but Emily says I can't wear it to school."

"Oh? Let me see it." Anything to take their focus off of Tricia. Would he have felt so attracted to her if he hadn't known she'd seen him naked? The idea should've embarrassed him, but he hadn't missed the way her eyes had studied him appreciatively. His bear grumbled its pride, knowing he'd put on a good show.

It didn't take but a moment for Oliver to grab his tablet and pull up the website. "This one. It's just a clown."

"Yeah, with blood splattered all over his outfit and a butcher knife in his hand," Duke replied. "Also, I'm pretty sure your school has a policy against wearing full-face Halloween masks to class. Yep, I'd say Emily was right." Just as he knew she would be.

Emily had raised kids and grandkids of her own and had excellent judgment, which was exactly why she was there.

Oliver's shoulders drooped. "Aw, man. I really wanted something scary."

"I don't want Halloween to be scary." Although she'd found another peach slice, Mia abandoned her spoon and slid down in her chair. "It was too scary last year."

Duke looked across the table at his daughter. She and Mason were only six, an age when Halloween should still be fun. The poor girl had been terrified the year before, even when there hadn't been anything to be afraid of. He knew she was still getting used to the loss of Lynne. Was it something she'd ever get past? "It doesn't have to be scary. And you're a whole year older now than you were last year, so you might enjoy it."

Mia's frown deepened.

"Why don't you tell me some things you *do* like about Halloween?" Duke suggested.

That got her thinking a bit. "Black cats. And carving pumpkins with you."

"We'll definitely do that," Duke said with a smile. "Maybe even a couple of them, and we can put them out on the porch."

"I like when you get all the decorations out of the attic, too." Mia had straightened up in her chair a little, now rolling her eyes toward the ceiling as she tried to think.

Emily joined them at the table. "You like doing crafts. I'm sure we can come up with some cute Halloween crafts to do, and you can add those to your decorations."

Mia was nodding now. "Yeah, and Ms. Simmons said we were going to have a class party with games and candy. Can I tell her I'll bring a bag of candy for the party, Daddy?"

"Of course." Duke would gladly fund the entire party if it would make her happy. Each of the children had been delicate in their own ways over the past year, and it'd been rough territory to navigate. Mia wore her heart on her sleeve and seemed to need the most support.

"I want to go to the haunted house," Oliver volunteered. He got up from the table with his bowl still full, but he sat back down when Emily pointed at his chair. "All the kids at school are talking about it. They've got all these awesome zombies and creepy things that pop out at you as you walk through."

Duke gave his oldest son a look but tried to be

subtle. They'd just gotten Mia past her initial fears, after all. "I think we'll have to talk about that later."

But children had a way of missing anything subtle. "I heard about that, too!" Mason exclaimed. "Joey said his older sister is working at it, and they're going to have a whole tunnel that's nothing but spiders and webs!"

"Boys..." Duke warned.

"Yeah! And there are huge skeletons in the trees and crawling over the building!" Oliver added.

"I wonder if there's going to be blood," Mason mused.

"Boys," he said more firmly.

They both glanced at their sister. "It's okay, Mia," Oliver said. "You don't have to go if you're scared."

But it was too late. She'd already seen just how enthused they were about the whole thing, and she wasn't about to miss out on something they were that excited about. "I'm not scared. I want to go, too."

"You don't have to, you know," Duke reminded her. "I can take Oliver and Mason, and we'll make sure Emily is available so you can stay with her. Or I'll see if one of your friends is free for a playdate." Duke had jumped at every invitation the kids had received lately, figuring the more they got out of the house and hung out with their friends, the better adjusted they'd be. It often ended up giving him a break, as well.

"No, I want to go," Mia insisted. "If they get to go, then I want to go, too."

Duke let a breath out through his nose. As a parent, it was often hard to tell what the right decision was. There were so many to make, and they came at him so quickly that it sometimes felt like he was dodging bullets. "We've got a little time before it officially opens, so we'll discuss it again. For the moment, the three of you need to finish getting ready for school."

With a clatter of chairs and the clanking of dishes, a small stampede cleared out of the kitchen and headed upstairs.

"Speaking of Halloween, you need to get yourself a costume," Emily said as she picked up her mug of coffee and took a long, slow sip.

"Hmm?" Duke glanced up at her sharply. "Why would I need a costume? They can wear their costumes when we go to the haunted house, but that doesn't mean I have to."

"I'm talking about the Halloween party at The Warehouse." The older woman pointed toward the flyer that hung on the fridge. "They're holding it early this year so it doesn't conflict with all the other things happening around town, and you've only got a few days."

Now it was Duke's turn to slide down in his chair. "Ugh. Do I have to go?"

Emily laughed. "Yes, I'd say you do. What would everyone say if the chief of police didn't show up? Especially when his own clan members are the ones putting on the event. Not to mention that the ticket sales all go toward the youth center."

"Fine." Duke knew she was right. There were all the reasons she'd already listed, plus the simple fact that he'd already said he would be there. "I'll go, but I won't enjoy myself."

"Won't *you* be a delight," she cracked. "Now then, what's Chief Grumpy going to be wearing to this party? Do I need to take you to the Halloween store when I take the children?"

"No, no," he insisted, straightening back up. "If people can dress up as police officers for Halloween, there's no reason I can't just wear my uniform."

She clucked her tongue at him. "You encourage your kids to have fun, and you ought to do the same for yourself."

"That's different," he argued. "I'd be happy to do almost anything they want to. We'll carve pumpkins, do crafts, and even bob for apples, but these parties are always kind of miserable."

"Life is what you make of it." Emily tapped the side of her coffee mug, which had that exact slogan on it. "And I knew that before I had this mug. You can sit around and be a bore, or you can get out and actually socialize."

"It's not like I have a lot of time for that," he reminded her. "I've got kids. They're my priority."

"As they should be, but what happens when they grow up?" she challenged. "They're young now, and it feels like they're going to be young forever. Trust me, they won't. They'll get their own lives about the time they hit high school, and then they'll get jobs. Girlfriends or boyfriends will take up a lot of their time, and the next thing you know, they're off to college. Meanwhile, you've spent so much of your time on them, you haven't got a life of your own."

He could certainly see her logic, even if he didn't like it. "Is this the voice of experience talking?"

She nodded. "Pretty much. I joined some book clubs and other groups and got past it, but it's still not an easy thing. You need to go to that party, and I need to go upstairs to do Mia's hair. You let me know if you need help finding a costume." Emily finished her coffee and left the kitchen.

Oliver had left his tablet on the table. Duke pulled it toward him and went back to the costume website, searching in the men's category. There was no way he was going to be a hot dog. It would be ironic and a little funny to dress up as a prisoner, but it probably wasn't a good idea.

With a sigh, Duke got up and headed to the primary suite to get ready for work. As he glanced out the bathroom window, his bear stirred inside him, knowing that Tricia was just across the field. The shade was down, and he couldn't see anything —not that he would've minded if he could. Duke imagined she was probably just dusting the light fixtures and digging through boxes. He shook his head. He had enough going on, and a sexy new neighbor was the last distraction he needed.

3

"I DON'T KNOW." TRICIA STOOD NEXT TO HER SISTER, looking in the mirror.

"Come on. It's perfect!" Tara insisted. She adjusted her beaded headband and reached over to do the same to Tricia's. "We look so friggin' cute! I thought these flapper costumes were to die for."

Tricia looked down at her body and shimmied her hips. "That's a whole lot of fringe."

"Isn't it great?" Tara leaned toward the mirror and fixed her eyeliner.

"I'm not sure if 'great' is the term I'd use." The blue dress, beaded headband, and long pearls would be cute, as long as they were on someone else. "I think you're just dressing me up for Halloween because you can't torture your kids with those itchy costumes anymore. Are you going to give me one of those pumpkin buckets and take me out trick-or-treating later?"

"Yup. And don't eat any candy until I check it for razor blades and needles," her sister teased. "Don't be such a stick in the mud." Tara flicked off the bathroom light, and they stepped out into the living room.

"I'm just not sure about this whole thing." Tricia picked up the small black clutch that she'd managed to find among her things. It sort of matched the costume, at least. She tucked her wallet and driver's license inside and was thankful that her phone fit as well, since the dress had no pockets. "I mean, why are we going? And don't give me that mom look. It might work on your kids, but not me."

Tara had tipped her chin down and pressed her lips together, but once she was called out on it, she stopped. "Fine. But you need to relax. It'll be fun. We're new in town, and we're never going to get to know anyone if we stay holed up in our houses all the time. I thought it would be a great way to network. In a small town like this, the success of your business can really depend on who you know."

Tricia sighed. "You're right. You're the only person I know up here, which means as of now, I'd only be able to sell one measly pumpkin." She peeked into the kitchen to make sure she'd turned off the light.

"You haven't met anyone else?" Tara challenged as she waited for Tricia to lock the front door. "Not one single person? Not even your neighbor?"

Her cheeks heated as she glanced toward Duke's house. She certainly had met her neighbor, and she knew quite a bit about him after getting that eyeful through the window. "Okay, one other person. I can sell *two* pumpkins now. I'll be rolling in the big bucks by Halloween."

"What are you going to do with this place, anyway?" Tara asked as they turned out of the driveway and headed toward the brewery. "I mean, I know Fiona left it to you, but that doesn't mean you have to keep it."

For some reason, the idea of selling the pumpkin patch and the old farmhouse got under Tara's skin. "You're keeping Cloud Ridge," she pointed out.

"Yes, and that's exactly why I'm going to this party. It's mostly been a turnkey operation, but I still don't know enough about this area or its people. I want to really embed myself in it." Tara headed around a turn in the road, tapping the wheel as her mind churned up business ideas. "I thought about doing something to celebrate the new ownership, but I want it to honor Fiona and the customers more than anything. Maybe I'll name a wine after her and plan some sales before the holidays. I'm not sure yet. I'm still figuring things out. You will, too."

As they pulled into the crowded gravel lot in front of The Warehouse, Tricia leaned forward to help Tara look for a parking spot. "I don't have a lot of time, though. I wonder if I *can* do anything with it this year, or if I'll have to wait until next season. I'm completely behind. What's so funny?"

Tara pulled swiftly into a space and threw the car in park. "I think you might be right about Fiona pulling one last prank. Neither one of us knows what we're doing. I mean, I've spent the last twenty years wiping chins, planning birthday parties, and shuttling everyone around between their activities."

"And now here you are, dressing me up, forcing me to go to a Halloween party, and shuttling my ass around."

There was a short line at the door where everyone was paying their cover charges. Tricia eyed the building while they waited. Its sign read 'The Warehouse,' and she could certainly see why. She was no architecture expert, but she guessed the old brick construction was at least half a century old, if not more. The tin roof was rusty in spots, and a few stray weeds stuck out along one corner of the building. If this ended up being a dump, she'd never let Tara live it down. The mouthwatering aroma of smoked meat escaping from the door was the only thing intriguing to her at the moment.

"Wow," she breathed as soon as they walked inside. "It's beautiful in here!" The brick walls remained exposed, but they looked incredible butted up against the gorgeous woodwork. The bar to the left looked like it was probably custom made, and it matched the old wooden floor perfectly. Even the beams overhead had finishing touches she wouldn't have expected. The enormous fireplace near the patio doors in the back gave the whole place a cozy feel. There was something else Tricia could sense in the air, a spark of excitement that jumped around inside her ribcage.

"Isn't it awesome?" Tara paid their cover charge and took Tricia by the elbow. "I stopped in earlier this week to have a peek. I mean, places like this are technically my competition."

"But they make beer, not wine." Tricia drew in a long breath through her nose. "And what I hope to be some amazing food."

"Let's find out." They joined the line at a buffet

along the back wall. Brisket, pulled pork, salmon, ribeye, and Italian beef were all being offered, along with fresh salads, roasted vegetables, and artfully arranged fruit.

"This looks a lot fancier than what I would've expected from a brewery," Tricia whispered. Maybe that little spark of energy inside her was due to hunger. Even if she hadn't been hungry before they arrived, she'd definitely want to eat after seeing this spread.

"And that's exactly why I'm saying they're the competition," Tara affirmed.

A young blonde woman in a tiny cat costume stood behind the buffet table. Her nametag said Daisy. "Hello, ladies! If you have questions about anything, feel free to ask. Don't forget to stop at the dessert table just over to your right. We've got some special Halloween candies in from Claire's Confections."

Tricia realized just how hungry she was. They quickly filled their plates and began looking for a table, settling on one not too far from the fireplace. "Fine," she said as they sat and she lifted her fork.

"What?"

"Fine. You were right in us coming here. Not because it's a Halloween party, and not because I feel like meeting people, but because of this food! I don't think I've eaten a proper meal since I got to Carlton, just sandwiches and a few cans of soup. I just haven't had the time, and I'm starving." She slipped a bit of brisket into her mouth and rolled her eyes into the back of her head.

Tara's shoulder sagged when she saw her sister's reaction. "It's that good? Great. I'm screwed. I was already worried about competing with the other wineries around here."

"The entire town can't fit into one business at once," Tricia reminded her. "Besides, people like to switch things up and try different places. Cloud Ridge is an established winery, anyway. You're not starting out brand new, so you already have some clientele. You'll be fine."

"And what about you?" Tara challenged as she cut into her ribeye, barely even needing a knife. "You've got an established business, too."

Tricia had tried not to think about the pumpkin patch too much. It was a bit of a cruel joke on her late aunt's part. Even though it was a relatively small establishment, she'd been too overwhelmed with moving and trying to figure out the rest of her life to research how to do this.

There was something about the air in the brewery, though, that was suddenly making her get into the Halloween spirit. It could have been the fact that everyone was in costume. Even the bartender had dressed as a pirate. Many of the costumed guests were sitting and enjoying their meals as she and Tricia were, but the staff had cleared the center part of the floor to make way for dancing. Tricia saw people laughing and smiling at each other, and waving across the room. There was a sense of togetherness and community there. That little spark in her ribcage was still there, as well.

"I do, and it might not take that much work to really make it into something," she mused. "I remember Fiona used to have the picked pumpkins arranged by size in the front yard, with little wooden signs that showed the prices."

"That's right," Tara said with a smile. "Simple and easy."

"But people want simple and easy in a different way these days. They want to take the whole family to one location and do a bunch of fun stuff. It'd be awesome to turn it into a fall family destination instead of just a pumpkin patch." Tricia's excitement churned. She'd spent so much energy on moving furniture and boxes, she was surprised she had any left for thinking. "It could be neat to have hayrides, or a little gift shop that sells homemade pies and other pumpkiny things."

"Look at you, getting all interested," Tara teased. "You'll be the pumpkin patch maven of Carlton before you know it."

"I highly doubt that. Like I said, I'll probably have to wait until next year. It's just a thought, but I think Fiona would enjoy seeing something like that happen."

"Not Uncle Dick," Tara noted. "He hated the fact that she ran a pumpkin patch there because it brought strangers onto his land."

Tricia almost choked on her brisket. "Yeah, he had a way of living up to his name, didn't he? It's hard to imagine someone as funny and sweet as Fiona being with an asshole like him. I guess you just never know who you might end up with. Speaking of, you're single now. Maybe you should cruise this place for guys instead of potential customers and employees."

"Speak for yourself." Tara smirked as she subtly pointed her fork across the room. "The phantom of the opera is over there checking you out."

Tricia forced herself not to look right away, but her curiosity got the best of her soon enough. She lifted her head and traced her eyes around the perimeter of the room, being sure to study the people in just about every other direction before she looked off to her left. There, not too far from the dessert bar that Daisy had mentioned, stood a man in a white half-mask. Even through it, she could see him looking right back at her. That spark in her ribcage instantly began acting up again, and this time, it ignited into a flame. It worked its way up into her throat as she realized she knew exactly who he was.

"Oh," Tricia breathed. "It's, um, it's my neighbor."

"*That's* your neighbor? Damn. I just assumed it was some crusty old farmer. Are you going to go say hi?"

"What?" Sweat erupted on her skin at the mere thought, and she felt like an idiot. She'd already seen him naked, and they'd even chatted in her living room, so it wasn't exactly a stretch of the imagination to go say hi. But that stare was so intense that she wasn't sure she could get out of her chair if she wanted to. "I don't want my food to get cold."

Tara nudged her sister. "You can always get more, and he looks like he wants to talk to you. Besides, he might be the perfect way to meet some other folks around here."

"I would say so, considering he's the chief of police," Tricia muttered.

"You're just full of surprises tonight, aren't you?"

"You don't even know." Tricia had nearly told her twin several times about what she'd seen through Duke's bathroom window. They'd always been close, and they told each other everything. This was something she wanted to keep just for herself, though.

"Well, you'll have to talk to him, anyway. He's coming over, and he looks like he's headed straight for you."

Tricia darted her eyes in his direction and saw that Tara was right. The last bite of brisket went dry in her throat, and she gulped down some beer to make up for it. Actually, she was probably going to need a lot of that tonight. Duke was just her neighbor. He'd politely introduced himself, and even after knowing that she'd seen everything she could want to see, he hadn't even tried to hit on her. There was no reason for her to be nervous, but that feeling inside her was now so intense, she didn't quite know how to control herself.

"Tricia," he said as he stopped at the edge of their table, those deep blue eyes staring so intensely into hers. "It's nice to see you again."

"Um, yes. You, too. This is my sister, Tara." She

made the introduction not only to be polite but hoping to take his gaze off of her for a moment.

"So I noticed," he said with a little smile as he nodded toward Tara. "It's nice to meet you."

"You, too. I'm surprised you could tell the two of us apart, especially when we're in the same costume. People get us mixed up all the time," Tara replied.

"There are some differences, even from across the room." His steady gaze was on her once again.

Tricia would have to remember to ask Tara why she'd said all that. It was true, but it only pointed out just how much attention Duke was paying to her, making the fire inside her spread down to her core. Most of the men she'd dated didn't really feel special. They were just other people with problems they wanted to add to hers. This was so different, it was almost painful.

"Would you like to dance?" Duke asked.

Adrenaline rushed through her veins, and her hand shook as she tried to hold onto her fork. She set it down and folded her fingers together in her lap, embarrassed at the idea that he could get her so frazzled. "Oh. Um, I don't know. It looks like it's kind of crowded out there, and I wouldn't want to intrude."

Across the table, Tara was glaring at her. She

kept darting her eyes to the right, toward Duke and toward the dance floor. After a few tries, she was even getting her head involved as she mentally told Tricia to get the hell out on the dance floor with this hot guy.

As if he'd also sensed her hesitation, Duke held out his hand. "Please? I'd hate for you to come to your first event in Carlton and for anyone to say I didn't welcome you to town."

Shit. As she lifted her hand from her lap, Tricia knew she was too scared to act on the choice she actually wanted. She laid her fingers in his palm.

His warm, rough hand immediately closed over them. He didn't yank her from her chair so much as he lifted her, as though she didn't weigh a thing, and they moved out to the dance floor.

Tricia was all too aware of every part of her body, down to the tiniest movements of the fringe that covered this silly dress, when Duke turned her to face him. He twined his fingers with hers and pressed his other hand to her lower back. When the music started, she was glad he was holding onto her. Otherwise, she might not have been able to stay on her own two feet.

4

SHE WANTED HIM. DUKE KNEW BY THE WAY SHE sucked in her breath when he touched her back, the way those deep brown eyes looked up at him, the irises full. Even her lips parted in anticipation.

His reaction to her told him everything he needed to know, even if he didn't want to believe it. It was too soon, too complicated, but the bear inside him seemed to think otherwise. It wasn't as simple as dancing and seeing where it led from there.

"I didn't expect to see you here tonight." But his beast had sensed her the moment she walked through the door. Duke had been prepared for a night of good food and some idle chitchat with the firefighters, police officers, and paramedics that he so often worked with. He wouldn't need to make excuses when he wanted to leave early, because everyone knew his situation.

Tricia took a breath before she spoke, moving her chest against his body. Their costumes provided several layers of material between them, but there might as well have been none. "And I didn't expect to be here. My sister dragged me."

"I guess that means I should thank her. I wouldn't have gotten to dance with you otherwise." The way her hips moved along with his was going to be his undoing. It was hard enough just to stand and talk to her, but now that he had his arms around her, he could barely control himself.

Her cheeks flushed, and she looked away slightly. "You don't have to flatter me like that. I'm more than happy to let you have whatever pumpkins you want, no charge."

Duke traced his eyes down to her dress. From his history classes, he knew the boxy style was supposed to make her look less feminine, but it simply couldn't hide her curves. The swell of her breasts peeked out at the top, tempting him with every sway. He moved his hand along her back so that he caught some of the fringe between his thumb and finger. "Is this how you're bribing me into not writing a ticket if you speed through town?"

"How could you do that?" Her eyes danced with challenge, and her free hand ran along the shoulder and lapel of his tuxedo jacket. "With this getup, I'd think you'd be driving a carriage instead of a squad car."

He laughed, hoping she wouldn't stop caressing him like that anytime soon. "Dragging my great-grandfather's tails out of the attic worked well enough for my costume. It was better than wearing my uniform, or so I'm told."

"I haven't seen you in it, but I'm sure it looks just as good." She caught her lower lip in her teeth as she studied him, as though she were trying to envision him wearing it.

"I'm afraid you have an unfair advantage over me when it comes to that."

She tipped her head to the side, causing the little feather in her beaded headband to flop a little. "How's that?"

"Well, I haven't exactly seen you parading around naked in front of your windows. It seems a little selfish not to have returned the favor." He meant it as a joke, but the mere idea had his bear lashing at the underside of his skin. He only had his imagination, but he was sure the reality of her was far better.

She arched a thin brow at him. "Maybe you could meet me out in the pumpkin field sometime for a private show."

The reaction that caused in him was hard to control. There was the raw, sexual attraction that he felt for her, the side that had known from the moment he'd laid eyes on her that he wanted her. Then there was that other part, the visceral need to protect her. Tricia clearly thought of her little plot of land as being completely isolated. She had no idea just how important that piece of land was to the clans, and the notion of her being that vulnerable threatened to drive him even more wild than having her body pressed up against his.

He forced a smile. "All the layers of this tux are making it hot in here. Would you like to step out on the patio and get some fresh air?"

"I suppose you would get hot, if you're used to not wearing anything at all," she teased. Tricia glanced at the glass doors at the back of the building. "I'm not sure if we're supposed to go out there, though. No one else is."

The music amped up, giving him the chance to lean down. He felt the heat of her body so close to his, and a wisp of her hair grazed his cheek. "It's all right. I know the owner."

She laughed, a shimmer of pleasure against his chest. "And here I thought you'd get away with it for being the police chief."

Duke shrugged as he straightened. "That, too."

Slipping through the doors, Duke took a deep breath of the crisp night air. The moon sent silvery light trickling down through the trees to dapple the patio furniture. Extinguished candles sat in the middle of each table, reminders of the gatherings that'd been happening there all summer. Now, leaves gathered on the chairs, and soon enough, the staff would cart everything inside for the winter. He thought the cool breeze might calm his bear and his desire, but when he looked down at Tricia, he knew he was wrong.

The pale glow of the moon picked out the high-lights in her hair, but it darkened her eyes. Every tiny movement made the fringe on her dress dance. "You look gorgeous tonight."

"You're not so bad yourself, although a tux is always a flattering option." Her eyes traced over his body appreciatively. "I'm pretty sure you have nothing to hide under that mask like the phantom did."

He swept the mask back, which only allowed him to see her all the better in the dim light. Her eyes moved up to his throat, across his jaw, and to his mouth. He felt that gaze as though it was her touch, and his lips were alive with energy. Duke bent his head, closing the small gap between them.

Tricia's lips were soft and warm, just as delectable as they'd looked from across the room. Duke explored them, the tenderness near the center, the thrill of each corner. He pulled back slightly, remembering that there was a whole brewery full of partygoers, any of which could glance through the patio doors and see them.

But just as their lips parted, Tricia lifted her chin to steal an extra kiss. Duke's bear swirled to life within him, seizing control and taking what it wanted. He grabbed her by the hips and pulled her closer, eliciting a squeal from Tricia as she crashed against his body. That noise echoed in his mouth as he kissed her again, the vibration setting his tongue on fire. He slid it between her lips, desperate to taste her.

Tricia opened up to him with a moan, tipping her head back and inviting him to explore her depths. She moved her hands across his chest, her fingers gently caressing the material of his tux and tucking in under the lapels. The texture of her tongue against his sent endless shivers of pleasure through his body, and he knew it wasn't just the chilly night that surrounded them. That damn fringe picked up those shivers and sent them racing back along his fingers. Duke tightened his grasp on her hips, knowing he was barely keeping himself under control.

Apparently, Tricia didn't want him to. She pushed up on her toes as she wrapped her arms around his neck. The movement made her breasts slide against his chest, and even through the layers of fabric that separated them, Duke could feel how luscious they were.

The ground was tipping underneath him. Duke led her backward into the shadow of the building and pressed her against the brick wall. It scraped his knuckles, but he would've bloodied them a hundred times if it meant he got to touch her like this.

His hardness throbbed as he ran his hands up over her ribs and to her breasts, the warmth, and softness of them tantalizing through her dress. He indulged himself in the way they reacted to every movement.

The party and crowd they'd left behind faded to a distant memory as Duke broke away from her lips and trailed his kisses down the side of her neck. Tricia pulled her arms down to keep them out of the way, her hands slipping down his waistcoat. Her fingers slipped under the hem, drifting along his waistband.

A deep growl of desire welled up from within him as Duke scraped his teeth along the delicate skin of her throat. Tricia gasped, but she pressed her hand along the placket of his zipper, encouraging the hardness that she'd created. Duke's hands immediately dropped, and he bunched up the skirt of her dress as he shimmied it up her thighs.

Tricia's breath was hot and fast as she yanked down his zipper and swept his shirttail aside until she could set him free. She wrapped her fingers around his shaft and stroked it as Duke found the delicate lace of her panties and yanked it aside.

"Fucking hell," he groaned. Her wetness only fueled his desire, and he couldn't wait any longer.

Sliding his hands up her bare thighs, Duke lifted Tricia, bracing her against the wall as he drove himself into her, and she shuddered, her hands clinging to his shoulders. Her panting breaths deepened with every stroke until they became impassioned sighs that matched the rhythm of his hips and told Duke he wasn't the only one enjoying this.

He closed his eyes as they pounded into each other, concentrating on the crisp, floral scent of her skin. She filled his senses, drowning out all the other chaos in his mind with the gasps emanating from her throat. He reveled in the way she squeezed around him, and for once his bear and his human were in alignment.

Tricia's fingers tightened against his shoulders as her breath quickened. Fire sizzled through him as he felt her core pulsing around him, drawing him deeper and demanding that he give her exactly what she wanted. Her convulsions intensified until her thighs were trembling against him and broken cries lifted into the air from her lips.

Duke covered her mouth with his to bury the screams that were starting to rise within her. As she came undone around him, Duke had no choice but to go along for the ride. Every muscle tightened and released as he flowed into her.

The world slowly seeped back into the edges of his reality. The breeze flicked at his hair and picked out the places where her lips had dampened his skin. His body felt heavy, as though his soul had slammed back into it too hard. His lips were raw and his muscles were tight. Duke lifted his head and met Tricia's gaze. He would let her go for now, but he couldn't ever truly untwine himself from her.

5

"YOU'RE UP EARLY, CONSIDERING THE NIGHT YOU HAD."

Tricia, bent over a cardboard box, instantly froze. "What do you mean?" she asked into her headset.

"I mean," Tara clarified, "you don't normally stay out as late as we did at that party."

"Right." Tricia straightened, taking a few books from the box and putting them on a shelf near the fireplace. She knew her exhaustion didn't have anything to do with what time she got home. Even once she'd showered and had gotten in bed, she hadn't been able to turn her mind off. She looked like a total wreck. "I'm a little tired today. Maybe it's a hangover."

"Then you need to build up your tolerance," Tara

advised. "I have a full menu of wines, but I've got to get a better variety, and I was thinking I should throw in some whiskeys and beers. That might attract more guys that otherwise wouldn't want to get dragged along with their wives and girlfriends."

Tricia reached back into the box. "Didn't you find anyone at the party who could be your taste tester? I thought that was the whole point of going in the first place."

"Apparently, the point was to be abandoned by my sister," Tara teased. "I lost track of you when you went off to dance with Duke."

Yeah. Dance. That was what they were doing. And she still had the scrapes from the brick wall to prove it. "I didn't mean to be gone for so long. I told you that last night."

"I'm just giving you a hard time."

No, that was what Duke had done. And he'd done a damn good job of it.

Tricia didn't even have to close her eyes to envision the feeling of him plunging into her, his hands under her ass as he'd held her up against that wall. It'd been raw and spontaneous, the kind of thing that happened to other people but not her. She'd gone on dates and joined guys at their places afterward or let them come back to hers, but even when it was good, it was never like *that*. Never had someone else's hunger for her turned her on so much. She'd seen the desire in his eyes and felt it in his body, and that was all it'd taken to send her straight over the edge.

Fortunately, Tara was far more interested in talking about Cloud Ridge than pinning Tricia down on exactly what she was doing with whom. "And anyway, I *did* meet people. I ended up talking to the bartender, who's actually the owner of the brewery. His name is Chase Thompson. I thought he'd be pissed when he found out that I owned Cloud Ridge, but he was actually really nice. He said he's been looking for a winery to do an exchange with."

"An exchange?" Tricia broke down the box she'd unpacked and put it in the stack with the rest of them. The place was looking a bit empty now that it wasn't full of boxes. There were still a few paintings and prints on the wall, but it needed a little something more. Tapping her teeth with a finger, she realized there was one place in the house that she hadn't yet explored.

"Yeah. People come into The Warehouse mostly for the beer and food, but sometimes they want a glass of wine. It's the exact sort of thing I was just talking about with bringing some beer or whiskey into the winery. This guy's partner Jenna is a marketer, and she thought it would be a great idea for us to work out a deal where we could feature his beer at Cloud Ridge and my wine at The Warehouse."

"That's fantastic." Tricia pulled the string to the ceiling trapdoor in the upstairs hallway. She stood back as dust rained down before stepping forward to pull down the ladder. It was ancient, but it seemed sturdy enough when she tried the bottom step. "If you hear a scream and a bunch of thumps, send someone to rescue me."

"What? What are you doing?" Tara was finally pulled far enough away from her talk of Cloud Ridge to pay attention.

"Just checking the attic for Halloween decorations." Tricia went up, slowly putting her weight on each step to make sure it would hold her before she proceeded to the next one.

"So, you really are getting into the pumpkin patch spirit." Tricia could hear the smile in Tara's voice, even over the phone.

"I think I'm also avoiding the last few boxes from

the move. I still haven't fully tackled the kitchen, and
I'm not sure I want to." She reached the top of the
ladder, but everything was pitch black. Tricia pulled
her cell out of her back pocket and turned on the
flashlight. "Wow."

"What is it? Oh, you shouldn't have gone up
there without me! There might be some great trea-
sures up there. You know, I always thought about
getting a booth at an antique mall. I love old dishes
and glassware, and I think I have a pretty good eye
for it."

Tricia made a face, wishing she'd realized she'd
get the 'I-wish-I'd-gone-into-antiques' speech again
by bringing her sister along on this little foray to the
attic. It was too late now. When her phone's light
illuminated a dusty switch to her left, she turned
it on.

Five or six dusty lightbulbs lit up. One of them
popped as the electricity fried its filament. There
was still plenty of light from the remaining bulbs to
see that Fiona hadn't just left her a farmhouse and a
pumpkin patch, but a bunch of other junk as well.
Trunks, boxes, and bags were stacked through most
of the space, but at least someone had the fore-
thought to put planks across the joists so she
wouldn't have to worry about falling through.

"Don't worry. Plenty of stuff will still be here for you to rummage through." The lightbulbs let her find her way around, but she still used her phone to read the faded old labels.

"Anything good?"

Spotting a box clearly marked 'Halloween,' Tricia opened it. The thick layer of dust on top suggested it hadn't been opened in quite some time, but everything inside looked practically brand new. "Cardboard cutouts of black cats, plastic pumpkins, a ceramic skull candle holder, and some artificial leaf garland. Yeah, I'd say I found exactly what I was looking for."

"There's got to be more up there than just old decorations," Tara insisted. "Maybe some vintage clothing?"

"I don't think I'll be getting through all of this right away, but I'm sure you can come help me when it's the middle of winter and we don't have anything else to do," Tricia assured her. "Oh, but I did find an old photo box."

"Really?" her sister squealed. "Please tell me there's an old one of Fiona. I've been thinking a lot about this wine that I'd like to name after her, and it would be so much fun to put a photo of her when she was younger on the label. I was going to ask

Mom if she had any, but I haven't gotten around to it."

Putting the carton of Halloween decorations over near the ladder so she could grab it easily on her way out, Tricia opened the top of the photo box. The lid lifted off easily to reveal not just photos, but an assortment of mementos. She pushed aside a packet of letters and a pendant with a family crest of some sort that she didn't recognize to get to a stack of black and whites down toward the bottom. What she saw made her laugh out loud.

"You're killing me over here," Tara reminded her.

"I'll have to send this one to you." Tricia took a quick pic of the photo and sent it over, but then she couldn't stop looking at it. Fiona couldn't have been older than twenty, and her big hair and mod dress were straight out of the sixties. She looked happy as she wrapped her arms around a bear, tipping her head so that she lay on its shoulder.

"That's not real, is it?"

"I don't know," Tricia admitted, "but it sure looks like it. Too bad we didn't find this when she was alive. It was probably at a circus or a zoo or something, not that anyone would let you do that these days."

"I think it'd be perfect for the label," Tara mused. "Will you set it aside for me?"

"Of course." Tricia paused, listening. A solid thump was resounding through the house. "I think someone's here. I'll talk to you later."

Leaving the boxes in the attic for the moment, Tricia descended the ladder as quickly as she dared. The knocking on the door was echoing in her heart, and as she hopped down into the upstairs hallway, she knew exactly why. It was silly. There was no need for her heart to be racing like that, nor did she need to be grinning like an idiot. Still, she couldn't stop herself from hoping it was Duke, standing on her porch. Maybe he'd want to have a repeat performance of last night, only this time they'd do it right there on the living room floor. Or he could be more of an old-fashioned guy and want to talk. Either way would be fine with her.

"I'm coming!" she called out as she barreled down the stairs, giggling at her own inadvertent innuendo.

But when she flung open the front door, she didn't find Duke. Instead, she saw a group of four men standing there. Her stomach flipped, and then she instantly tried to correct herself. Just because she lived out there in the middle of nowhere didn't mean she needed to worry if some random strangers showed up on her doorstep. In fact, this was probably a lot more common out there. She swallowed and put on a smile as she stood on the threshold. "Hello."

"Hi, ma'am. I'm Charlie Johnston." The man closest to the door reached out to shake her hand before he gestured behind him. "This is Brian, Brandon, and Caleb. Our family owns the land behind you."

"Oh." That knowledge was all the proof she needed that this was a simple courtesy call, and it wasn't really any different from Duke stopping by to say hi to his new neighbor. "I'm Tricia Fitzpatrick. It's nice to meet you."

"You too, ma'am. I understand you haven't been here very long?" Charlie had bright blue eyes, but there was a certain spark to them that made Tricia uneasy. Duke's deeper blue eyes radiated warmth and desire, but this man looked like he was assessing her.

Tricia didn't like it, but she reminded herself it was probably because she didn't know them. "No, I just moved in this week. I hope to have the pumpkin patch open soon enough, though."

The one Charlie had introduced as Brian, a man who was also similar to her in age, took one long drag on the end of his cigarette before he flung it into the front yard. "I don't think we'll be buying any pumpkins."

"Could you please not do that?" she snapped quickly. "I don't want my yard full of trash."

"I'm so sorry about that," Charlie said before the other man had a chance to retort. "Brian, go pick that up out of the nice lady's yard, please."

Brian grumbled as he slunk down the porch steps and searched for the butt among the last remains of the gladiolas while the two younger men laughed. They looked to be in their early twenties, still full of too much energy and testosterone. Brandon's curly brown hair seemed to only sprout from the top of his head before wildly flinging itself down over his pimpled forehead. Caleb had the hood of his sweatshirt pulled up over his ears.

An uncomfortable feeling settled in the pit of Tricia's stomach, and now she wished she hadn't jumped off the phone with her sister. "It was nice of you to stop by, but I really do have some things I need to take care of. Pleasure meeting you." She stepped back and started to close the door.

"Actually." Charlie put out one meaty hand,

spreading his fingers wide against the wood and stopping the door from closing with little effort. "There's something we wanted to talk to you about."

Her jaw tightened, but he clearly wasn't going to give her a choice. "Yes?" she asked icily.

Charlie gave her a condescending smile that hinted he knew something she didn't. "Much of the land in these parts has been in my family for generations. As I said, the farm just behind you is ours. So is the one off to the west. Even the land that your little place here is on had been ours once. You might know Fred Johnston?"

She was pretty sure she didn't have a clue, and at this point, she just wanted them to leave. "I don't believe so."

Another smile from Charlie. "It was his brother who used to own this place, Dick Johnston. Fred is my uncle."

Tricia supposed that made the two of them some sort of distant cousins by marriage, but she wasn't going to bring it up. "And? I'm sorry. I really have a lot going on right now."

"My apologies, ma'am. I just wanted to let you know that I'm interested in buying the property from you. We'd like to get all the family land back together, and we'd be more than happy to take this old place off your hands."

"Yeah, it's kind of falling apart." Brandon poked the toe of his shoe at a small hole in one of the porch floorboards.

Anger flared inside her, along with a possessiveness of the land. "That's *my* problem to deal with. I'm not interested in selling."

Charlie tipped his head to the side and quirked up his eyebrow as though he thought she was making the wrong decision. He ran that fleshy hand through his short gray hair. "Well, you just let us know when you change your mind. Come on, boys." With a simple gesture, he had them all casually heading down the stairs, scuffing their shoes in the gravel driveway as they headed back to the old red truck they'd parked there.

Tricia shut the door and immediately locked it. "What assholes! *When* I'm ready to sell, my ass! I've already given up my chair rental in Eugene and brought all my shit out here with me, and it's not like I'm going to just run off and buy some other place."

A shot of adrenaline still ran through her blood, making her shake. Tricia leaned against the door, waiting for the feeling to stop. It really was a rundown old place. There were tons of things that needed to be fixed, and it'd probably keep her busy for decades to come. Still, it was hers. Fiona had left it to her, and even if it was just a prank, Tricia liked to think it was for a reason.

6

DUKE BRACED HIS HANDS OVER HIS KEYBOARD AND had his eyes on the screen, but his mind definitely wasn't on work. He sat up in his chair, took a deep breath, and forced himself to concentrate. Being a police chief meant he constantly had something to do. There were schedules to be made, investigations to be conducted, and court appearances to coordinate. Several evaluations were due, too. Not to mention the flood of reports that his officers had to turn in to him on a daily basis. Hell, he was even in charge of ordering cleaning supplies. It wasn't as though he had time to slack off, and he sure as shit didn't expect any of the men and women who worked under him to slack off, either.

Picking the easiest task for the moment and

clicking over to the office supply website, Duke's focus instantly vanished as soon as he added paper clips to the cart. They weren't nearly as exciting as what'd happened between him and Tricia. She'd been so damn hot in that dress, and the slightest movement of her body had sent the fringe flying out toward him. How could she have expected him to resist her? *Well,* he thought with a smirk, *maybe she didn't.* She'd been more than willing. Tricia had kissed him back with a ferocity that sent lava flowing through his veins, evaporating any thoughts of resistance. Her gentle moans in his ear and the way her legs had wrapped around him were further proof.

It was exciting, yes, but it was also something else. Not quite terrifying, and not exactly shameful, but somewhere in between. First of all, he was in a leadership role within the community. If anyone found out that he'd fucked a woman up against the side of a building at a Halloween party, he might very well lose his position. It was certainly consensual, but it still wasn't the kind of thing the city council would appreciate.

Then there was the matter of dealing with Tricia herself. He'd made no commitment to her. He hadn't gotten down on one knee or asked her to move in with him, but Duke still wasn't sure how to act. He'd drawn the curtain over the bathroom window before he'd showered that morning, and he hadn't even spent time out on the porch or in the yard for the last couple of days. It was driving his bear crazy to know she was that close and that he'd had his bare hands on her hot skin, yet he was keeping himself as far away as possible. It might not be a problem for other men, but it was a new one to him.

"Good morning, everyone!" A curvy woman with curly brown hair stepped into the office, carrying a baby seat over one arm and a lunch cooler over the other.

Officer Landon Scott had been frowning at his computer as he typed in a report, but his face had instantly transformed into joy and love as soon as he looked up. "This is a pleasant surprise! What are you doing here? I thought you had to take the baby to his doctor's appointment."

"We're on our way right now, but you left your lunch on the counter. Again." Michelle kissed him as he came around the desk to greet her.

Duke watched two little feet kicking out from the baby seat as they talked. His children might all be old enough to go to school now, but it didn't seem like all that long ago that he was trying to keep socks on their feet or getting up in the middle of the night.

He got up from his desk since he wasn't getting any work done, anyway. "How's the little guy doing?"

Michelle eagerly turned the seat so Duke could get a better view. "He's an absolute doll, but I guess I think that even when he's screaming like a banshee in the middle of the night."

Duke reached out a finger. Every baby did it, but there was something so heartwarming about having those tiny fingers wrap around it. Baby Corey had the dark hair and eyes of both of his parents, but it was hard to tell which one of them he would truly end up looking like. He kicked his legs excitedly to see so many people around him. "He's a cutie. Just wait until he starts crawling. Then you won't be able to keep up with him anymore."

"That's all right. He's already giving me plenty of exercise," Landon replied with a proud grin. "You didn't tell me just how exhausting it was to have kids."

"You wouldn't have believed me, anyway. I know I didn't. When Oliver came along, he slept like an angel and hit all of his milestones just like he should. I thought babies were easy. Then we had twins." He shook his head, knowing that said it all. Even easy babies were a lot to handle when there were two of them.

"I've got to get going, so we're not late for the pediatrician. It was nice to see you, Duke. Bye, honey." Michelle gave her mate another warm kiss before she and the baby headed out the door.

Landon watched them go, standing there with his hands on his hips and pride on his face. "It's really something, Duke."

"I know. I'm glad things have worked out so well for the two of you. Most of the time, when an officer arrests someone, they don't end up having a baby and moving in together," Duke teased as he headed for the coffeepot.

"True enough. Just remember that your kids are quite a bit older than little Corey, which means I'll be coming to you for advice all the time." Landon grabbed a mug for himself.

Duke shook his head. "It's not like anyone is really an expert on it. Kids are all different, and we're all different. What I do with mine might not work out for yours. I'm still constantly trying to figure things out. It's only gotten harder, too."

"I'm sure it has," Landon said quietly.

He slowly stirred half and half into his coffee. "I know you had some reservations about getting together with Michelle. I mean, because of the issue with children."

A curse had afflicted Landon's family that brought out the worst of the shifter side in their first-born male children. In fact, his older brother Corey had been under its influence for the last few decades before some local witches had intervened. "I was lucky enough that we got that taken care of."

"Kids make everything more complicated, though. I mean, if it was simply a matter of you and Michelle wanting to be together, it would only be up to the two of you." Duke considered the box of doughnuts that someone had brought in, but he didn't think his stomach could handle the sugar right now.

Landon narrowed his dark eyes at his boss. "You're not usually one to beat around the bush."

"Yeah." Duke sighed and glanced around. The other officers were out on their patrols, and dispatcher Sean Moss was closed off in the back. "I know you had a lot of things to consider when you and Michelle met, and it's not quite the same situation, but it might be a little relatable."

"That bush isn't going to have any leaves left on it," Landon warned.

"Okay, okay." Duke pinched the bridge of his nose. "I met a woman."

Landon clapped him on the arm. "That's great!"

"No, not really. I mean, she is, but it's just not that simple. I feel so guilty about it." Saying that last part out loud made him realize just how much the guilt had been weighing him down over the last few days. He hadn't felt like himself at all, and he didn't know how to fix it.

The other officer studied him. "I have some ideas, but why exactly do you feel guilty?"

"I haven't been with anyone since Lynne," Duke admitted. "I know there are plenty of people who suffer a loss like that, and they deal with it by going out and losing themselves in a bunch of flings, just like they do when they get divorced. I never felt like that, and I honestly didn't think I'd ever be interested in someone else again. I'd already found a mate in Lynne, so why would anyone else matter?"

Landon tapped his fingers on the table. "It may be bold of me to say so, but I think Lynne would want to see you happy."

Memories flooded back to Duke, ones that weren't easy to relive but refused to leave him alone. "She told me as much before she died. The cancer took her quickly, but we had some time to talk."

"You don't have much to worry about, then."

"But what about the kids?" Duke argued. He balled his fist and slowly pressed it against the nearby doorframe. "They're my priority. My *only* priority. They come above everything else."

"That doesn't mean you don't still have your own needs or that you don't deserve to be happy," Landon reminded him. "I know I haven't been at this parenting thing nearly as long as you have, but Michelle and I know we can't just work and be parents. We need time alone and time with each other. It seems selfish, but we can't be the best parents we might be unless we take care of ourselves. It's the whole oxygen mask thing."

"What?"

"You know, when you get on a plane and they go over the emergency procedures, they tell you to put your own oxygen mask on before you take care of the child or elderly person next to you. You can't help them breathe if you can't breathe yourself." Landon took a long sip of his coffee.

"It's not a bad analogy," Duke admitted.

Landon shrugged. "I can't take any credit for it. It's been around for a while, and now it's all over social media."

"That explains why I haven't seen it, then. I don't do much of that, although I'm sure once Oliver hits junior high, he's going to be all over me about it. That and about a million other things. I just don't know if I honestly have the room in my life for someone else." It wasn't as though he and Tricia had even talked about such things, but he knew the potential was there. If he consulted his bear, it was more than just a potential. It was an absolute.

"So, this woman... is it more than just attraction?"

They both knew how it felt, the pull of their true mates. Fate had a way of putting them together, making sure they could find each other across space and time. It was up to them to do the right thing about it, but the animals inside them were persistent. Duke had felt it once before, so he couldn't question it the same way someone might if they were experiencing it for the first and perhaps only time. "I thought I'd be miserable with anyone other than Lynne, and now I'm miserable because I'm trying to stay away from her."

"That should tell you something right there." Landon topped his mug off. "You're a good dad, Duke. Everyone in town knows it, and that's one reason everyone likes you so much, even though you're a total hardass."

"Get back to work and stop gossiping around the coffee machine," Duke replied.

"Yes, sir." Landon gave him a mock salute as he headed back toward his desk.

Returning to all the work that awaited him, Duke knew there was wisdom in what Landon had to say. His kids were important, but so was he. They wouldn't want him to live like this.

Their school pictures from last year sat in matching frames on the edge of his desk. Soon enough, he'd be swapping them out for this year's pictures. Oliver had an over-exaggerated smile on his face, trying too hard. Mia looked sweet and hopeful, just as she always did. Mason had a little spark of mischief in his eyes, and Duke wondered where that would lead as he got older.

They were wonderful kids. They were his whole life. Even if Duke managed to balance his time between them and a relationship, how would they feel about it? They still needed him so badly, and he knew he needed them, too. It wasn't an easy thing to figure out, and all the advice in the world wasn't going to help. It was something he'd have to decide for himself, but there was nothing saying he'd have to do that right away. There was time, and he had enough on his plate.

7

"Okay. You're next." Tricia moved her wheelbarrow down the narrow path. She'd found that Fiona had strategically planted these rows to have just enough room between them to get in and work without wasting space. The paths were the same width as the wheelbarrow, and somehow, she'd trained the vines to run in the right direction so they wouldn't get squashed by the wheels.

Kneeling down, Tricia inspected the trailing plants. They didn't look like much at this point, just miles and miles of prickly fuzzy vines that didn't look capable of sustaining the big orbs that were growing from them. She wished she knew what she was doing, but at least she had the internet. Being careful not to disturb the shallow roots, Tricia plucked out a handful of weeds.

"I know a lot more about hair than pumpkins," she said to a plant as she grabbed a shovel full of compost from the wheelbarrow and delicately laid it around its base. "I guess it's not really that different when you think about it. You have to take care of it and make sure it has plenty of nutrients in order to grow, and if you put the wrong chemicals on it, you're going to burn it up."

Tricia laughed softly at her corny joke. She'd worried about making the wrong decision, but right now, she wasn't missing the long hours of gossip back at the salon. One woman would come in and complain about her friend, fully expecting Tricia to agree with her. Then the friend would be in later that week, making the same complaints about the first woman. She loved many of her clients, but some were straight-up energy vampires, leaving her emotionally exhausted by the end of the day. Then there were all those hours on her feet, sometimes with very few breaks to make up for late clients or to fit in as many appointments as possible, making sure her chair rental didn't go to waste. The manager expected her to promote expensive products, and she never knew just how much she would make in tips.

Out there, the fields were peaceful. The autumn sun was warm on her shoulders, and Tricia was surprised to find she actually enjoyed getting her hands down into the dirt. It was kind of fun to take care of something, trying to figure out the best way to get it to grow. There was no telling if she was going about it the right way, but she was trying. That was all she could really ask of herself, and she'd find out soon enough when it was time for the pumpkin patch to open. She'd even left her cell phone in the house so she could completely disconnect from the hubbub of modern life and simply enjoy nature.

Though she'd been trying to avoid it, Tricia glanced to the side at Duke's house. She hadn't heard a single word from him ever since their tryst at the Halloween party. Not that there was any reason she should expect to. They could be mature adults who just had a little fun, and that was okay.

But then why had he looked at her so intensely when he'd come across the room to her at The Warehouse, as if he hadn't been able to help himself from coming to see her? And why had her body reacted so deeply to his? She'd fallen into his arms as though she'd known him for a lifetime, and she hadn't regretted what they'd done together for a second.

Except that now she had to wonder if he was avoiding her. Tricia hadn't done anything wrong as far as she knew. Duke had seemed to enjoy himself just as much as she had, so it wasn't that. But his curtains had been drawn, and she hadn't even seen him heading out of his driveway.

Tearing her glance away from his house, she tried to focus on her work. Getting the pumpkin patch up and running was her priority right now, and she wanted to at least have the chance to honor Fiona's memory by selling a few pumpkins this year. Her late aunt had probably done a much better job with this, and if she could see Tricia trying to arrange the vines without breaking them, she'd likely laugh at her, but she was still going to give it her all.

A shadow fell over the plant she was working on. Tricia looked up to see a man standing over her. He was backlit by the sun, and so she couldn't discern his features. He didn't give her that nervous excitement in the pit of her stomach, so she knew it wasn't Duke. As she shielded her eyes from the sun, she saw the newcomer had three other men with him.

Standing up, she came face-to-face with Charlie Johnston.

"Hello," she said politely, determined not to let him know just how much he'd gotten under her skin the last time he'd come over. "It's a beautiful day, isn't it?"

"Indeed. A very nice day to sell this property to me." Charlie leveled his gaze at her.

"Um, not exactly." Clearly, he thought he could intimidate her until she did what he wanted. Maybe if he'd asked to buy the land as soon as she'd known about her inheritance, before she'd actually moved out there and made her meager attempts to work the land, she might've considered. But this had been one of Fiona's favorite hobbies. Her aunt hadn't needed the money. Cloud Ridge had brought in more than enough income for her. She'd always talked about her pumpkins and how fun they were to grow. Charlie could claim a family attachment to this property, but so could she.

Charlie shook his head and clucked his tongue. "You know, you're really in over your head with this place."

"You don't know anything about me. You don't have a clue what I'm capable of. It's not like it's that damn hard to grow these things." Or so she hoped. She lifted her chin a little, aiming to look like she meant it. Charlie didn't need to know her agricultural education was limited to what she'd learned on sleepless nights on her phone. She'd read several articles and watched a few videos, but it certainly didn't make her an expert. At least Fiona had already started the work for her by planting the fields back in the spring.

"Oh, no," he laughed with that same condescending smile on his face. "The fields are one thing, but you could always pay someone to till those under and turn them back into grass for next year if you didn't want to bother with them. There's also the house itself. Word is, it needs to be torn down."

"I think that's between me and the home inspector. For the moment, it's just fine." Hell. She hadn't had the place inspected, but she probably should. She'd put it on her list, but she wasn't going to tell Charlie about it.

"The wiring is bad. The whole place could go up in flames one night." He grinned as he made an upward gesture with his hands to show just how quickly it would happen. "You'd be out here, all alone, and no one would know about it. You wouldn't even be able to get the fire department out here fast enough to save it. For that matter, you might not be able to save yourself."

She knew a threat when she heard one, but she highly doubted they'd actually do anything. People were full of talk, but Tricia knew better than to worry too much before someone gave her a legitimate reason to. She folded her arms in front of her chest. "I think I'll manage."

Charlie took a step closer. He had a wide face, but his cheekbones and chin were prominent enough that he looked like his own Halloween mask. His eyes twitched as he studied her, looking for signs of intimidation. "Did anyone warn you about the dangerous creatures that live in the woods in these parts?"

It took all of her self-control not to look over his shoulder and into the tree line. She and Tara had visited Fiona there when they were children, and though she'd let them roam anywhere they wanted in the pumpkin fields, they'd been warned never to go into those woods. What did Charlie and Fiona know that she didn't? "I'm not scared of a few raccoons. It seems to me that the only pests around here are the four of you."

Charlie started laughing, a low and menacing sound that slowly grew to a roar. "You have no idea!"

"What do I need to do to get you off my property?"

"Simple. Just sell it to me. Then it will go back to the Johnston family, where it should have always stayed. Then you can carry on with your little gardening projects anywhere you want to. I'm sure you can grow some pretty flowers in a window box somewhere."

Tricia had tried so hard not to let this guy get under her skin, but he'd finally pushed her past the tipping point. "Listen, I—Hey! I already asked you not to do that!"

The scruffy one named Brian had once again finished a cigarette and flicked the butt. This time it'd gone sailing off into the pumpkins, and it'd be impossible to find among the leafy vines. Brian didn't look the least bit sorry as he grinned and shrugged his shoulder. "Yeah, and we asked you to do something, too."

Charlie let out another laugh. "He's got a point, you know."

"These things don't look so good." Brandon had his hands in the pockets of his sweats as he braced his foot on top of a pumpkin. He stepped up onto it with both feet and bounced his heels down. The rind split easily, sending a cascade of gooey orange guts out the front while Brandon stumbled backward to regain his footing, laughing the whole time.

So was Caleb. "Hey, you're right. I mean, look how weak they are." He lifted the heel of his boot and easily stomped it into the next pumpkin. A spray of seeds burst out over the aisle, and he went for the next one.

"What do you think you're doing?" Tricia charged toward them. "You can't do that!"

"We can do whatever the fuck we want," Brandon replied as he kicked the remains of the pumpkin he'd destroyed, sending half of it flying. "It's not like you're going to stop us."

"The hell I'm not!" Rage had bloomed inside her, an anger that instantly boiled. She didn't know exactly what she was going to do, but her mind wasn't even slowing down to think about it. She only knew that she was going to stop this asshole.

"He's right." Brian stepped in front of her, blocking her from getting near the destruction they were causing. "I mean, what the fuck were you thinking, lady?"

She narrowed her eyes, hating him with the full force of her being. "I think you fucking reek, and you might want to take a shower before the flies confuse you for the compost pile."

"Bitch." In one swift movement, Brian lifted his hands and shoved them into her shoulders.

Tricia lifted a foot to step back, but one of the many pumpkin vines snaking through the area caught her heel. She waved her arms, but it was no good. Keeling over backward, she tried to catch herself, but the metal wheelbarrow came up and slammed right into her back. She'd landed near the handles, and the cart unceremoniously dumped her on the ground. When her palm hit the hard earth of the pathway, a snap zinged up her arm and exploded behind her eyes. It pulled all the breath from her lungs as she collapsed into a pile on the ground. The world reeled around her, a confusing mix of sky and dirt.

She felt the distinct thud of booted feet as Charlie came and stood next to her. His silhouette blocked out the sun completely as he bent down, leaving her feeling cold. "Consider this your last warning, unless you'd rather be doing all your gardening from the wrong side of the dirt."

He turned to leave, or at least she supposed he did. Tricia couldn't see him, nor could she turn her head to try. Her body hadn't yet decided to cooperate. She could hear the distinct smashing of pumpkins as their low voices slowly retreated.

The air slowly seeped back into her lungs, but having the ability to breathe again didn't dull the ferocious pain in her arm. Tricia knew it was broken, even before she dared to look at it. The flesh was already swollen, and she thought she saw a tinge of purple on the surface of her skin. A wave of nausea rolled through Tricia as she lifted her eyes from the wound, wanting to think about anything else at the moment. There was a reason she hadn't become a doctor or nurse.

She concentrated on a nearby pumpkin, one that hadn't been smashed. It was a larger variety, the kind that would be perfect for carving as long as the Johnstons allowed her to keep it alive. Before she'd been so rudely interrupted, Tricia had carefully turned the ungainly fruit, being careful not to snap the vine in the process, to keep it from getting flat on one side. She'd then placed a bit of plastic mesh under it to keep it off the ground and prevent rot. They were little things, tips she'd read and had thought to be far too much work. Now, she'd much rather be pulling weeds and turning pumpkins instead of lying there, wondering just how the hell she was going to get out of this field.

Maybe she never should've come out there at all. Tricia carefully rolled over onto her back, sucking air through her teeth as she accidentally moved her arm. She noticed the sky was bright and lovely with a few wispy clouds streaking through.

It was a beautiful day. A beautiful day for having regrets.

8

"HERE'S MY LATEST REPORTS, CHIEF." OFFICER Brecken Hewitt put a file on Duke's desk. "Nothing particularly exciting today."

Usually, Duke would think that was a good thing. Right now, he could've used the distraction of a big investigation or a drug bust. "Thanks."

Brecken turned to gather his things and head out at the end of his shift, but he paused. "Are you okay?"

"Sure," Duke replied automatically. "Why?"

"You just seem kind of tense, that's all. I thought maybe you had some concerns about Halloween." Brecken rubbed his jaw with one hand, scratching his fingers through the pale stubble.

"Hmm? No. I don't anticipate anything happening." There had been a few mishaps on Halloween here and there: teenagers smashing pumpkins, egging houses, and bombarding trees with toilet paper. Sure, parties got out of hand on occasion, but for the most part, trick-or-treaters filled the streets, and the police had a heavy presence to make sure they were available if anyone needed help.

"Trouble on the border?" Brecken pressed.

Duke's stomach pushed back against his spine, although he couldn't be sure why. He'd lived on the border of the Johnston and Thompson territories for a long time. It was his duty to watch for disturbances and handle them before they escalated, just as it'd been the duty of the generations before him. That vigilance and the observation skills that came with it had made him a natural police officer, and he'd climbed the ranks without really meaning to.

He wasn't aware of trouble between the two clans at the moment, but the idea made him uneasy. "I don't think so, but I'm going to check on some things. Will you do me a favor before you go and let everyone else know I'll be in my car instead of at the desk?" Duke grabbed his keys.

"Sure thing." Brecken headed into Sean's office.

Behind the wheel of his squad car, Duke found the agitation growing inside of him. It dug deep, poking the bear at his core. He knew it'd been quite some time since he'd let it out, so maybe that was his problem.

As he headed out of town, though, he became less convinced. Something was wrong. He could feel it in the marrow of his bones. That inner turmoil only grew as he got closer to home. He'd felt this before, back when Lynne had taken a downturn. He dialed Emily, ready to hear her assurances that everything was all right. The ringing echoed through the car, making him feel more hollow by the second. His stomach was in his shoes by the time it clicked over to voicemail. He hung up and hit the gas.

Duke tore into the driveway. His heart was a lump in his throat, but it couldn't turn off his instincts as an officer. His eyes traced over every detail of the house as he threw his car into park, watching for anything out of place that would give him a clue. Gauzy ghosts swung lazily in the breeze from the porch railing. The wreath on the door was slightly crooked, but it always got that way after the door had been opened and closed several times. There was no sign of anyone as he pounded up the stairs and burst through the door. "Emily? Kids?"

"We're in here." Emily leaned out the kitchen

doorway, her forehead wrinkled with concern. "What's wrong? What is it?"

"That's what I came to find out." He strode into the kitchen to find all three kids seated at the table with coloring sheets and a big pile of crayons in the center. Scissors and scraps of construction paper lay to the side, and someone had dropped the wrapper from a Rice Krispy treat onto the floor. Everything looked completely normal.

Duke's shoulders sagged with relief. "I tried to call you," he managed to say. He wasn't even sure if he'd said it loud enough to be heard over the thundering heartbeat in his ears. "You didn't answer."

"Oh." Emily picked her cell phone up off the counter. "That's odd. I never heard it ring, and it doesn't say there's a missed call. I think I need to call the company. I've been having some problems with it lately."

"You do that." Duke leaned in the doorway. His family and home were fine. Nothing had come through dispatch, and he still had his radio on him, just in case. Why was he still feeling like this? His bear urged him to act, and it'd become even more desperate once he got home.

"Daddy, look! I made a witch!" Mia proudly held up her coloring sheet.

"That's very nice, honey." His senses were on high alert, and his vision had sharpened. He could see every stroke of crayon she'd put on the page.

"You need to make her look mean, like a real witch," Mason advised.

Emily put her hand on Duke's arm. "Are you all right?"

"*I* am, but something isn't. Give me a minute." Duke stalked through the house. Whatever made him feel this way wasn't far. He just had to find it.

Though no one should've been in the primary suite since he'd left that morning, Duke flung the door open anyway. Everything was as it should be, but the tension in his shoulders only ratcheted up. He peeked into the bathroom, just in case. He'd accidentally left the cap off his shaving cream, but otherwise, it was just as normal as the rest of the house. Frustrated, he turned to leave when something caught his eye.

That morning, Duke had opened the curtain on the window before he'd left the house. He was already fully dressed and didn't need to hide behind a piece of fabric just because he didn't know how to deal with his feelings for her. Part of his own yard was visible through the glass, with the pumpkin field on the other side. The dark green vines were beginning to pale as they put their energy into the pump-kins, but he noticed a bright splash of color that didn't belong there.

Duke raced back out of his bedroom and into the kitchen. "Emily, keep the kids inside and lock the doors behind me."

She blinked, startled. "Of course!"

"What's wrong, Dad?" Oliver tried to follow him to the front door.

"There's no time. I'll talk to you later." Duke was on the porch in a flash, his feet hardly touching the stairs before he was in the yard. They carried him straight toward his goal as his eyes scanned the trees lining the back side of the properties. His senses were overflowing with information as he tried to understand the situation. There was no doubt in his mind that something terrible had happened, and he couldn't be convinced it wouldn't happen again.

Hurtling into the pumpkin field, Duke barreled down the aisle until he reached the wheelbarrow. It'd been turned on its side, and as he skirted it, he saw that the odd patch of color in the field was exactly what he'd feared it was. Tricia lay on the ground, her purple flannel shirt and jeans smeared with dirt. She was as pale as the white pumpkins growing on the back side of the property, her lips dry and thin.

His bear was overwhelmed with rage and concern. Duke knelt next to her, gently touching her face. "Tricia. Tricia, wake up. You need to tell me what happened. Are you injured?"

She nodded slightly as her eyes fluttered open. Tricia stared at him for a moment, looking confused. "Hey," she finally said.

"Where are you hurt? What happened?" he demanded. Duke's bear was whipped into a frenzy now. He began checking her body for injuries, feeling along her shoulder and down her ribcage.

"That tickles. Ow!" She let out a scream of pain as she tried to move out from under his hands. "I think my left arm is broken."

"How did that happen?" Duke moved over to inspect her arm, his hands moving without much input from his mind. He was sure her assessment was right, and it was probably painful as hell, but at least nothing else appeared to be wrong. Duke carefully lifted her arm and laid it across her stomach. Undoing the last few buttons of her flannel, he flipped her shirt's hem and refastened it to some buttons further up, creating a temporary sling. It wasn't pretty, but it would serve while he got her onto her feet. "Did you trip or something?"

The pain was bringing her out of her stupor. "No. It was... never mind. It was nothing." Tricia let out a moan of pain as he helped her sit up, then she slumped over against his shoulder. She pressed her head against him for a moment, just breathing.

He couldn't say he minded how it felt to have her need him like that. When she leaned against him, Duke thought he could hold up the entire world. But that fantasy shattered as soon as he looked beyond Tricia and saw the smashed pumpkins, broken vines, and churned dirt around them. Several large boot prints had been pressed into the soil, and his anger was now beyond measure.

"Don't give me that bullshit." Anger was bubbling inside him, overriding the raw sexual desire from simply being near her. Duke had always been able to put his feelings aside when he was dispatched to a call. His job as a police officer had nothing to do with whether or not he liked the person he pulled out of a wrecked vehicle or if he agreed with someone about a dispute. It was about getting people to safety and upholding the law. Right now, though, he felt far less like a police officer and more like a rabid, possessive bear. "What the hell happened?"

"Some guys showed up, and –"

"*Who?* Who did this to you?" As his gaze intensified, he felt the prickle of fur emerge at the back of his neck.

"Charlie Johnston and some other rednecks." She let out a small laugh.

Duke failed to see even the smallest amount of humor in this. Those bears had a death wish, but right now, his priority was taking care of Tricia. "Let's get you to your feet, and then I'm taking you to the hospital."

He had more than enough strength and adrenaline to get her upright, but it was clear by the way she was walking that she wouldn't make it to the car. "Did you hit your head?"

"A little, but I'm just woozy. I don't like blood or anything... *medical.* I don't even like talking about how it bothers me." She leaned harder into him, and her breathing increased.

"I'm going to bring you over to your driveway, and then I'll get the car and come over here." Duke wrapped one arm around her waist and the other around her legs, sweeping her up into his arms. Her ponytail flopped over his shoulder, and she pressed her cheek into his chest. Duke gritted his teeth, reminding himself she only needed him this much because she was injured, and he was the only person around. Anyone else would've done the same.

Reluctant to leave her for even a second but feeling he had no choice, he put her on a bench under a tree not far from the driveway. As he gently set her down, he felt regret ripple through his body. "You stay right here. I'll be back."

At her nod, he dashed back through the field and his yard, glad he still had his keys on him and didn't have to run into the house. Emily and the kids would wonder what was happening, but he'd have to fill them in later. They were used to emergencies of all kinds, which meant they were also used to waiting for information.

It was only a short race down his driveway and over into hers, but Duke spent the entirety of it berating himself. It was his duty to guard this section of the border, a job he'd been performing for quite some time now, but obviously, he'd dropped the ball. Yes, he still had to work and take care of his family. He couldn't be there all the time, and no one expected him to be. But clearly, the Johnstons had discovered he wasn't infallible, and they'd finally decided to start some shit. Why did it have to be now? And why with Tricia?

Gravel crunched under his tires as he braked to a halt, as close to the bench as he could get. His patience was wearing thin, but he waited until he had her buckled in safely. They were on the road before he spoke again beyond murmured assurances.

"Tricia, I know you're dizzy and in pain, but I need to get the story from you. If Charlie Johnston is responsible for this, I have to do something about it." Let her think he was talking about charging and arresting the assholes. What he really wanted was to tear every person remotely responsible limb from limb with his bare teeth. He could almost taste the blood as he turned off the side road. Duke flicked on the lights but not the sirens. He needed to hear every word.

She tilted her head back against the seat, cradling her broken arm with her good one. Her eyes were closed, and she licked her lips. "I'll try to recall it the best I can. Charlie, Brian, and a couple of younger guys came onto the field because Charlie wants me to sell him my property."

Duke nodded, his knuckles white on the steering

wheel. "They wanted it back in their family, I'm sure."

"Yeah. I'd already told him no when he'd tried pressuring me into it before, but he thought he could come back and change my mind." Tricia lifted her good hand to rub it against her forehead.

"Wait." If this hadn't been an emergency, he would've slammed on the brakes and pulled the car over. "He'd already been pushy with you, and then you went out and worked in your field by yourself?"

Tricia cracked one eye open and looked at him. "Well, yeah."

"But that's dangerous," he argued.

"I didn't think it would come to *this*." She gestured at her flannel sling with her chin. "What was I supposed to do? Just hide in my house?"

"You should've told me about this." To think he could've prevented this only made him more frustrated. He should've seen it coming. There was no way that Dick and Fiona Johnston's land could simply be passed on to a human without someone trying to intervene. "It's my job to handle things like this, you know."

"I know it's your job, but can you do me a favor and please just let it go? I'm new in town, and the last thing I need to do is make this a bigger issue than it should be."

"What's stopping them from doing this again?" he snapped. "Or maybe something even worse?"

"Look, don't get mad. I really don't want to press charges and draw more attention to myself. I just want to move on with my life."

"I'm not mad at you," he replied, although he could certainly see why she thought he was. She was injured, lightheaded, and probably scared, and he was yelling. He was angry, but not at her. He was angry with the Johnstons for always putting their agendas above anything else, even the safety of others. He was angry with himself for not noticing that trouble was brewing. Most of all, he was angry that he'd distanced himself from Tricia after they'd hooked up at the Halloween party. How could he have expected her to come to him when he'd been trying so hard to stay out of her way? He'd pulled back, and she was the one who had to pay the price.

Duke swept in front of the emergency room doors. The staff saw the squad car, and two workers immediately emerged with a gurney, ready for whatever he'd brought them. "I'm pretty sure her arm is broken, although she may have hit her head, too."

They swiftly put Tricia on the gurney, even

though it was probably overkill, and nodded. "We've got it from here, Chief."

"I'm staying, actually," he said as he entered the doors behind them. Tricia would likely be safe there, and he had no doubt that the staff would get her all the medical treatment she needed, but he couldn't leave.

He'd already left her once, and this happened.

9

"I CAN'T THANK YOU ENOUGH FOR THIS." TRICIA closed her eyes as the warm water cascaded through her hair and gurgled into the sink. There was something comforting about those sounds, even though she'd decided the chaos of hairdressing no longer had a place in her life.

"Of course you can. In fact, I'm pretty sure you already did. Don't you remember when you came and painted my toenails while I was pregnant?" Tara grabbed the conditioner, put a big dollop in her hand, and slowly began massaging it in. "Having the portable salon chair and sink sure makes this a lot easier."

Tricia smiled. "I almost sold it before we left

Eugene because I didn't think I'd ever need it again. I didn't want to haul it all the way up here if I wouldn't use it but thank god I decided to keep it. Trying to wash my hair with one hand was driving me crazy."

"Remember when you used to make me play salon with you when we were little?" Tara turned the water back on and spoke up to be heard over the noise of it. "We made such a mess out of the kitchen sink. We'd get Strawberry Shortcake shampoo, conditioner, and water everywhere. Mom never really got mad about it, either. She just reminded us where the rags were and said it had to be cleaned up before she needed to start cooking dinner."

"Clearly, you learned a thing or two since you practically wash hair like a pro," Tricia noted.

"I wish you'd forced me to play winery with you instead. I could sure as hell use a little more knowledge under my belt. Sit up." Tara squeezed out the excess water and wrapped a towel around her sister's head. "Do you want me to blow dry it?"

"No, I'm just going to let it air dry." She let out a satisfied sigh, knowing her hair was fully clean again. It was a small thing, but it felt damn good. With the towel still around her head, she got up and went to the fridge for seltzer water. "What's wrong at the winery?"

Tara accepted the can Tricia handed her as they moved to the living room and settled on the sofa. "Nothing exactly, but I just don't feel like it's right. One of the waitresses put in her notice because she's getting married and moving to New York. She shouldn't be too hard to replace, but the idea of being short-staffed for any amount of time is freaking me out a little. I've gotten the impression that Cloud Ridge has been running like a well-oiled machine, but now that I've come along, it's starting to fall apart."

Tricia shook her head. "I think you're imagining that."

"I don't know. There's just so much to take care of, and I'm not sure I'll ever keep up. Between the staff, the fields, the finances, advertising, and all of these laws I have to figure out, it's a lot. And no matter how hard I work, there's always more to be done." Tara frowned a little as she took a sip of her water. "How about you?"

"You're kidding, right?" Tricia pointed at her arm, all trapped in its cast. "How am I supposed to pick all these pumpkins and get them into the front for sale? Kick them like soccer balls? I thought about just letting people come and pick their own, but I don't think I want them stomping through the fields."

Tara grinned. "You really are getting attached to this place, aren't you?"

"Surprisingly." She was restless and annoyed and needed something to do, so Tricia headed to the kitchen for a bag of chips. Her brain was buzzing about the pumpkins, the farmhouse, her arm, and everything else that'd happened since she'd moved to Carlton. And the worst part? She couldn't do a damn thing about most of them.

"You could always hire someone. I bet some kids in town would be happy to make a few bucks lugging pumpkins around." Tara reached into the bag for a handful of chips.

Tricia chewed thoughtfully. "I considered that, but my finances are already running kind of tight with moving and quitting my job. I'm just living on my savings until I can open this place, but that doesn't seem all that likely right now."

"Sure it is. If Fiona could keep this up and running for all those years, there's no reason you can't. And what happened to all those fun ideas you were talking about just a week ago? You had big plans for this place," Tara pointed out. "You already said you probably wouldn't have time to transform the farm this year, but you might be able to do it by next year. You sounded really excited about it."

"Yeah," Tricia admitted. She started to reach into the greasy bag for another handful but changed her mind. They weren't really helping. "But that was before our dear distant cousins by marriage decided to threaten my ass."

"Oh. That's what this is all about." Her sister nodded her head sagely.

"What?"

Tara shrugged as if it were all so simple. "You're just allowing yourself to let go of the idea of the pumpkin patch because you're worried about what Charlie Johnston and his dufuses might do. You're pretending you don't think you'll be successful so you can't be disappointed later."

Tricia frowned. None of that was wrong; it was all pretty obvious, but that didn't mean she enjoyed hearing her twin point it out. "Maybe. I don't know. The fact is that I'm not capable of doing any of it this year, and I'm not sure there's much point in trying if I'm just going to be harassed by my neighbors constantly." She grabbed a throw pillow and propped her broken arm on it.

"Don't let those assholes stop you," Tara encouraged. "They're just a bunch of bullies. As I recall, you didn't put up with any bullshit from Laura Massey."

"That was in high school," Tricia reminded her. She unwound the towel from her head and tossed it across the back of a chair for the moment. "All I did was step between her and that poor foreign exchange student and call her out for having a knockoff bag. It was small potatoes compared to what we're talking about here."

"Okay, fine. But you can get this taken care of. You do also have the police chief living right next door. I almost keeled over when you called and told me what'd happened. I still can't believe he stayed at the hospital with you. That was really sweet," Tara said with a smile.

"Yeah, well, I was pretty dizzy. You know how I get when it comes to doctors and hospitals." Tricia knew it was more than that. Duke was doing his job when he'd scooped her up out of that field and taken her to the hospital. He would've done that for anyone. But would he have carried them against his chest like that? And would he have stayed at the hospital, insisting on getting her anything she needed and then driving her back home? He'd even gone through the entire house to ensure it was safe before he finally returned to his place.

She could feel that there was something between them. Though she'd never been one who necessarily believed in destiny or fate, it was hard to ignore the magnetic pull between them. He'd been furious that she was hurt, and she'd been so relieved to see him. Hell, the guy had even pulled pumpkin seeds out of her hair while they'd waited for the doctor. All of that had to say something, yet she could tell he was keeping his distance. There was something else at play, something she didn't understand.

"All I know is that I think we belong here. Fiona wanted us in Carlton for *some* reason," Tara theorized. "I think she knew that if she left us these businesses, we wouldn't just sell them. She shook up our lives. Most days, I feel so far behind that I might as well be stomping grapes with my feet, but at least I'm not sitting around at home, moaning about my kids not needing me anymore."

"I'm glad you're feeling good about it, but I just don't think I can right now. I'll try, but I can't make any promises." Tricia sipped her seltzer water, suddenly wishing it was a glass of wine. She'd had a hard time relaxing since her encounter with Charlie. Knowing that he and his thugs lived so close by didn't help.

Content to let the subject drop for the moment, Tara nodded her approval. "Oh, do you still have that photo of Fiona handy? I need to get it to the graphic designer so we can get started on the label."

"It's over here." Tricia had nearly forgotten about the box of mementos she'd pulled out of the attic. She shivered a little, telling herself it was just her damp hair on her back, not the memory of the first time Charlie had shown up at her door. She crossed the room to the mantel.

"I've got it." Tara rushed over to help so that Tricia wouldn't try to grab the box herself. She lifted the lid and took out the packet of old letters. "What is all this stuff?"

Tricia shrugged. "A bunch of family drama about people we don't know. I've read through some of them, but it's hard to keep track of it all when I only see the letters from one side. Basically, it sounds like a Johnston boy was engaged, but the girl broke it off, and then everyone got all riled up about it."

"If the Johnstons were anything like they apparently are now, then I don't blame the poor girl," Tara joked.

Tricia laughed. "I know. It's the kind of stuff you'd see plastered all over social media today, but I guess a hundred years ago, they just used to write long, angry letters about it."

"Are they really that old?" Tara carefully put the packet of papers back in the box.

"They seem to be. It's kind of funny to feel responsible for keeping the history of a family that I don't belong to and that wants to kick my ass, but I also can't bring myself to throw them away. It's the same way I feel about this house and land. I know we visited Fiona here before she built her other place, but I'm not all that sentimental about it. Something about the idea of people trying to take it triggers this possessiveness in me, though. Oh, listen to me. I must be getting tired."

"I'm telling you: Fiona wanted us to be here. She was a crazy old bat, and maybe she didn't do it for anything other than a laugh, but there was still some sort of reason," Tara affirmed as she tucked the old photo safely into her wallet. "I've got to get home so I can get up early and head to work. Are you sure you're okay here by yourself?"

That was something Tricia hadn't been entirely sure of since Duke had brought her back from the hospital. She'd kept her doors locked, and she'd often found herself peering through the windows to see what kind of dangers might lurk outside. But there was still that connection to the land that kept her there. "I'll be fine."

"Okay. You call me if you need anything. Or call your neighbor." Tara winked. "I'm sure that's what you'd rather do, anyway."

"What's that supposed to mean?" Tricia followed her to the front door.

"Come on, Trish. I'm your twin. We don't have to say things out loud for the other to know about them. Besides, you get that goofy look on your face every time I mention his name, so I know *something's* going on there."

Tricia squared her shoulders indignantly. "I do not."

"Yeah, you do." Tara slung her purse over her shoulder and looked at her sister with mischief in her eyes. "Duke."

A shiver ran up her spine, and that bloom of adrenaline shot through her body, but she pressed her lips together and forced herself to stare neutrally at her sister. "See?"

"I sure do," Tara replied with a triumphant grin. "Good night!"

"Good night." Tricia shut the door. How dare

she? Nothing was going on between them. Sure, she'd felt some sensual energy every time she saw him. And she'd had a glorious tryst with him behind a brewery. She could even admit he'd been a knight in shining armor when she'd broken her arm. But that didn't mean anything. If it did, more would be happening between them than their random run-ins.

Tricia padded back into the kitchen and poured herself a glass of wine, a nice Moscato from Cloud Ridge. She took it to the living room, where she sat in the wingback chair by the fireplace. The room was illuminated only by a couple of corner lamps at the moment, making it cozy. How many generations had sat there, wondering how the harvest would be? Did they have the same attachment to this place, a seemingly random connection that made them love the way the knots in the floorboards made odd little faces? Did they admire the brickwork around the fireplace, even though that one brick was slightly askew?

This little pumpkin patch was becoming such a big part of her life, and Tricia had never expected it. She realized as she sat there, with her arm broken in the name of keeping this piece of land, that she might not have intended to settle there permanently when she'd moved away from Eugene. It could be a rest stop, a respite from the unsettled feeling that seemed to follow her around before. Now that she'd felt it for what it truly was, she wasn't sure she could ever leave.

Starting to feel a little braver, Tricia got up and unlocked the door. She opened it a crack, peering out onto the front porch. Tara was long gone, and all was quiet and still. A cool breeze moved through, turning her damp hair chilly. Crossing over to the corner of the house, she leaned on the railing as she looked out over her pumpkin patch.

It was impossible not to lift her eyes just a little and study the warm yellow rectangles of light that shone from Duke's house. When would she run into him again? Because Tricia was fairly certain she would. Granted, neighbors were bound to see each other every now and then, but this felt different. A little thrill bubbled in her stomach.

Her eyes were dragged back down to the pumpkins when she noticed movement. It was dark, with only a touch of moonlight, but someone was definitely down there. Tricia clutched her glass of wine a little too tightly as she took a step back. Had Charlie returned, this time in the dead of night when there were fewer chances for someone to help her? What might he be willing to do to get this land away from her if he'd already had no problem leaving her with a broken arm?

Just as her fear threatened to take over, her eyes began to adjust. Whatever was down there wasn't big enough to be Charlie, or any other man for that matter. She blinked and leaned out over the railing a bit. Three small creatures were moving about amongst the pumpkins, exploring leisurely. Dogs? Raccoons? Either way, they didn't belong in her pumpkin patch.

Tricia set her wine glass on the patio table. The broom was still leaning against the siding where she'd left it after sweeping leaves off the steps. It wasn't much of a weapon, and she could only wield it one-handed.

She smiled a little as she imagined what Duke might have to say if he looked out his window and saw her plodding out into her field with a broken arm and a broom. He'd said he wasn't angry with her, but Tricia wasn't stupid. Duke might be furious with the Johnston men for doing such a thing to her, but it was clear that he also felt she'd put herself in danger. He was an officer of the law, and she could tell herself that he'd just seen too many people put themselves in bad situations. Was that it? Or was it something else?

As she reached the edge of the pumpkin field and had a better view, Tricia realized these weren't dogs or raccoons at all. The small dark creatures had round ears and long snouts. Their little hunched backs were covered in thick fur, and she could see their eyes glittering in the night. Bears. Three bear cubs. Her heart fluttered with surprise and joy. They were the cutest things she'd ever seen! Two of them appeared to be the same age, as they were the same size. The third one, a bit further back in the field, was slightly bigger. None of them had noticed her yet.

She might have stood there and watched them for quite some time, enjoying the stillness of the night and the peace of seeing nature at its best if she hadn't realized what they were doing. Their claws were short but sharp, easily slicing into the pumpkins, and together with their teeth, they made holes big enough to stick their snouts into. Triumphantly, they lifted their heads as they gobbled the insides, with strings and seeds clinging to their fur. When the bigger bear thought one of the smaller ones had gotten too close to his find, he rolled his pumpkin away where he could enjoy it privately.

It was adorable, but they were eating her profits. Tricia had already lost some pumpkins due to the Johnstons, and while she didn't begrudge the bears a bite to eat, she still needed to make this little business as successful as possible if she was going to have enough money to make it through the winter.

"Go on," she called out into the night, advancing down one of the aisles and lifting her broom in the air. "Shoo! Get out of here!"

The bears looked up. They stopped what they were doing and stared at her, the moonlight reflecting off their eyes, but they made no motion to leave.

"I said go," she encouraged, taking several more steps forward and being careful not to trip on a vine. The last thing she needed was to take another spill out there and break the other arm. "Go home, wherever that is. Go find something else to eat."

Finally realizing she was serious, the two younger ones scrambled off. With a huffy grunt, the biggest picked up the remainder of his pumpkin in his mouth and trotted off after them. They retreated into the darkness of the woods behind Duke's house and disappeared.

Tricia turned back for the house, smiling and shaking her head. The little bears were endearing and simply doing what wild animals did. As she neared her porch, she remembered that the mother bears were usually nearby and didn't appreciate having their cubs messed with. She dashed up the stairs and into the house, just in case.

10

DUKE DRUMMED HIS FINGERS ON HIS DESK. HE PICKED up a pen, twirled it, and set it back down again. He shook the mouse to wake up his computer monitor, finding several reports he still needed to do, but his brain wasn't interested.

It didn't seem to be interested in anything, actually. The last few days had all felt the same, as though he were just sitting around and waiting for something to happen. That wasn't a good feeling for his shifter side at all. It made him feel useless and irritated. Usually, Duke would consider heading out into the woods on Thompson property and taking a nice long run. Sometimes there was nothing like feeling the wind in his fur and his lungs full of fresh Oregon air. It was easy to get caught up in the day-to-day life of his human side, and it made that wild half of him all the more desperate to come out.

He hadn't done it, though. Duke was afraid of what would happen if he did. It wouldn't be a simple run, and he knew it. One possibility was that he'd head straight over to the Johnston land and immediately destroy whoever he could get his claws into, whether they were innocent or not. He wasn't even sure what it would take to stop him once he started.

Duke was just as likely to go find Tricia. The woman had a grip on him that he couldn't explain. It was attraction, of course, but the incident in the field had shown him it was so much more than that. It was impossible to close his eyes—or even blink— without seeing her lying in that field. He felt like someone had injured his own, which scared him just as much as knowing she was hurt.

Duke had already found his mate. Plenty of other shifters still hoped to do the same. How could he possibly be tied to someone else? And if so, how could he explain that?

Annoyed, he tried once again to put his mind back on track. She was all right now, and there was no need to think about this anymore. The doctors had assured him that her bones would heal and that she didn't have a concussion. Tricia was fine. Duke just wasn't sure that *he* was.

Like a caged animal, Duke knew he would snap and do something stupid if he didn't get out of this office. He pushed himself back from his desk and stomped over to the dispatcher's desk. "Anything going on that I need to know about, Sean?"

Sean turned from the bank of computer monitors in front of him and took one side of his headset off his ear. "Landon just went out to do a welfare check on a senior citizen, but everything was fine. Brecken pulled someone over for speeding downtown, but other than that, things have been pretty quiet."

Duke put his hands on his hips and sighed. Quiet days meant they could catch up on paperwork, and of course, that the town was also safe and peaceful. That was the goal they always strived for, but right now, he needed something else. "All right. Thanks."

He turned to head back to his desk just as the phone rang. Duke paused at the door as Sean answered it with his headset. "Carlton Police. Yes, ma'am. Is anyone injured? I'll send an ambulance and an officer out right away."

"What is it?" Duke was already reaching for his keys.

"There was some sort of confrontation in the grocery store parking lot. The call was from a bystander who said a woman was injured by an irate male. She didn't know all the details, but I could hear a lot of screaming in the background."

His bear twisted inside him. "I'm going to check it out. Send someone out there if they're closer, but let them know I'm also coming." Duke was out the door before he could wait for Sean's reply.

Out of the building and behind the wheel of his squad car, Duke cursed himself as he turned on the lights and sirens and screeched out onto the street. He'd hoped for a distraction, but he should've been more careful about what he wished for. What if this woman was Tricia? The Johnstons had already been bold enough to come on her property twice, even though she was right next door to him. What would keep them from assaulting her again, this time in public?

His bear seethed inside him as he pressed harder on the accelerator. The Johnstons were cavalier when it came to the safety of human lives, and they didn't even try that hard to keep the shifter secret under wraps. He could easily envision them attacking her right there in the parking lot in the light of day, not caring about the consequences as long as they got what they wanted. Tricia hadn't been scared off yet, but a person could only handle so much.

Once again, his mind drifted back to that hospital room in the emergency ward. The staff had jumped quickly to help, but they were always pretty good about that. Usually, he'd be looking for the shifter doctors who understood a different physiology was at play and would keep their mouths shut. He didn't have to worry about that this time since Tricia was undeniably human, yet he was still relieved to see familiar faces. Dr. Gaines was one of the best in town, and Meryn Stafford was a sweet and understanding nurse. They'd tried their best to make Tricia comfortable, but she'd still gripped his hand as they'd set the bone.

Duke made a hard right into the grocery store parking lot and forced himself to slow down. Two cars were parked in the middle of one of the aisles, angled and askew. He slammed his vehicle to a stop and got out, quickly moving toward the scene and trying to assess exactly what was happening. None of the cars looked like Tricia's, but he had no idea what her sister drove.

A woman—who definitely wasn't Tricia—stood near a cart corral just in front of a red car. "Look what you did, asshole! You completely busted up the front of my car!"

The moment Duke turned to assess the other individual, his bear thrashed inside him. Of all people, Charlie Johnston stood nearby, his fists balled at his sides. "I didn't do a damn thing, lady! You busted your own car when you swung into that space too fast and hit the cart thingy!" He motioned angrily toward the metal bars of the corral.

"Which I wouldn't have had to do if you weren't trying to steal my space!" the woman retorted. "I got here first, and I have it fair and square!"

As Duke approached, he took another look around just to make sure he hadn't missed anything. Tricia wasn't anywhere to be seen. "Can someone tell me what's going on here?"

"He tried to steal my parking spot!" the woman pointed her finger.

"Hey, lady. I had my turn signal on, and I was getting ready to pull in the spot when you came charging in here!" Charlie's face was already red, and now it was beginning to turn purple.

Duke steeled his jaw. "I was told that someone here was injured."

"Yes, I am!" the woman declared. "It's my neck, and it's all his fault!"

Charlie made a derisive noise. "You look like you're just fine to me, lady."

She twisted up her face in what was supposed to be a threatening countenance of warning, but it only made her look even more comical. "I already had an old injury from a previous accident, and now you've set it off again! Hell, you probably caused something else to happen, too!"

"Right. Pretty convenient for an accident that happened at five miles an hour," Charlie retorted.

Though he hated to admit it, Duke knew Charlie had a point. "The ambulance will be here shortly, and they'll check you out. Another officer's pulling up to take over from here, but in the meantime, step over here, Mr. Johnston. I'd like a private word with you."

"Can you believe this crazy bitch?" Charlie said with a laugh.

"Listen," Duke's words came out in a low growl. "I've heard about your visits to my new neighbor's property."

"You mean *my* property?"

Duke grabbed Charlie by the collar. "I'm going to say this once and once only. If you and your underlings step as much as a foot onto her land again, you're not going to get off on a mere trespassing violation. You'll be signing your own death warrants. I will end you right then and there. Understood?"

"Yeah. Whatever you say, man."

Landon had arrived and gave a quick nod to his chief. "Officer Scott will take things from here." Duke turned and headed back for his vehicle.

He'd gotten to the scene quickly, not only because it was his job to, but because he'd convinced himself he'd once again find Tricia needing him. He was relieved that she wasn't involved in the accident, but he wished he could have seen her. He wanted to feel her head on his shoulder, leaning into him not only with her physical body but with her soul.

He'd fallen for her. Duke had tried to fight it. He'd told himself that it simply couldn't be, and that even if there was a connection, it would be too complicated to deal with. His heart—and his bear—didn't care about complications.

Cruising back toward the station, he knew he was going to have to do something about it.

11

"You don't have to do this, you know. You've got a lot on your plate, and I don't want you to take up a bunch of time just because you think I need some inspiration."

"Stop it," Tara chided from the driver's seat. "It'll do both of us a little good to have a break, but I think this might help you get excited about your pumpkin patch all over again."

"It's not that I'm *not* excited," Tricia tried to clarify as they turned north of town and headed out into the country a bit. "I'm still going to stay there, and I still plan to try to get the place open this year. I just know that there's only so much I can do with what limited time and resources I have right now. It probably doesn't help that some bears came and tried to eat my inventory last night."

"What?" Tara's eyes widened as she turned to look at her sister.

"Keep your eyes on the road!" Tricia warned, laughing. "It's not nearly as bad as it sounds. They were little ones, just babies."

"I didn't think you liked baby anything." Tara checked the GPS to make sure she was still going in the right direction.

"That's not true," Tricia retorted. "It was right after you left. I went out on the porch, and there they were. I had no idea that bears liked pumpkins, but they sure seemed to enjoy them. I chased them off, though, because I still need to have enough of them to sell. Then I started looking up videos of bears eating pumpkins online, and I guess it's a thing. There are zoos all over the country that give them out as treats, and the bears go nuts. It was actually a pretty nice way to spend my time while sitting around with this broken arm."

One of Tara's infamous mischievous grins spread over her face. "Does that mean you're in the Halloween spirit again?"

"It means that I haven't given up," Tricia correct-ed. "Just don't get your hopes up that I'm going to suddenly turn into Superwoman and make everything happen in a day, okay? I already feel like I'm getting pressure from Aunt Fiona from beyond the grave, and I don't need pressure from you, too."

Turning off the highway onto a side road with a big sign that read 'Haunted House This Way,' Tara shook her head. "I wasn't trying to put pressure on you. I guess I just know how hard this has been for both of us, and you seem to be having a little extra trouble. I want to be here for you, that's all."

She would've reached over to squeeze Tara's shoulder if her broken arm wasn't throbbing at the moment. "I know you are."

It was early in the evening, but the haunted house's parking lot was already filling up. Tara found a place easily enough, though, and they walked up. "Do you remember when we tried to do that haunted maze back when we were kids?"

Tricia had to laugh. "You were so terrified, I thought you were going to shit your pants. I had to practically drag you through it."

"I thought we'd never get out of there, and they'd close the whole place with us stuck in it." They joined the line, which moved at a stilted pace to allow the groups to space out. Skeletons had been arranged all over the building to look like they were scaling the siding and peeking in the windows. "I still remember that nice lady at the end who was dressed as a witch. I thought she was the prettiest person in the world, but that might've been because she gave me an extra piece of candy when she saw that I was crying."

"There's no candy at the end of this one for you," Tricia reminded her, feeling a familiar old thrill as they paid their fee and stepped through the doorway. They were in a room that looked like an old Victorian parlor, lit only by electric candles that reflected out of the silvered mirrors. It was dim and dusty, and the door straight across from them was locked. They had to find another way through.

"That's all right with me. I had to get a little less jumpy once the kids got old enough to come to these sorts of things. They scared the hell out of me at first, but it got a lot better. Agh!" Tara had found a door that opened, but it only contained a zombified proper Victorian lady who lifted her curled hands into the air and growled.

The contrast between her grisly makeup and gorgeous mourning gown had Tricia laughing already, and so did her sister's reaction. By the time they found the right door, she was grinning and holding her stomach. "So you got better, huh?"

"Shut up! Oh. Ew." They'd come upon what might have once been a hallway but was now a tunnel full of spiders. Webs coated the walls and ceilings, and dim lights showcased the eight-legged forms that covered them. There were spiders of every size, from the tiniest little things all the way up to a massive tarantula down at the end.

"Come on." Tricia hooked her good arm through Tara's and led the way. "At least you know they're all fake. Okay, maybe not."

"What?"

Tricia pointed to a glass case that'd been set into the wall. It was a terrarium, and several live spiders were crawling around in it.

"Ewww!" Tara shrieked. "I wish you hadn't shown me that! Let's go!"

They quickly made their way out of the spider tunnel and into another dark room. This one had been arranged like a filthy old kitchen, with fake blood and moldy meat everywhere. An animatronic butcher stood in the corner, his eyes blinking as he slowly lifted and lowered a cleaver.

"Promise me that whatever you do with your pumpkin patch, you won't have anything that's spider-themed," Tara said as she tried to catch her breath. "That was terrifying."

"Is this room all right?" Tricia asked.

"It's just the same sort of stuff you'd find at the Halloween store, so yeah." Tara let out a nervous laugh. "I honestly didn't think anything here would bother me. I guess I was just being brave for my kids, and now I need you to be brave for me!"

Still grinning, Tricia shrugged. "I don't mind. This has actually been a lot of fun, and we're not even done yet. Let's see what's through here." The black door at the end of the room had 'Enter if You Dare' written on it in fake blood. She dared, all right, and she opened it.

The other side appeared to be pitch black. Tricia knew they didn't allow anyone to use their flash-lights or phones in there, so she took a careful step forward. A brilliant strobe of green flashed, showing a wall of black fabric in front of her. Another strobe blazed a moment later, this time in red.

"What is this?" Tara was still clinging to her right arm, her fingers intertwined with Tricia's.

The next flash was blue and a bit dimmer, but it showed an opening on the left. Tricia stepped forward. "It's a maze."

Tara's shiver went all the way up Tricia's arm. "You're kidding me, right?"

"Nope." It was not only a maze, but one that was

almost completely dark. The random strobe lights made it all the more disorienting, and Tricia knew that her sister was being instantly transported back to that maze they'd been through as kids. Just as it was then, she knew the best way to get through this was simply to charge forward and start trying.

Tara stumbled along behind her. "You know, there's probably someone around who can just let us out the side door. I think they're required to have some sort of emergency procedures like that."

"We're fine," Tricia assured her. She'd had a lot of moments lately when she hadn't felt very brave. Charlie Johnston and his crew had scared the hell out of her, and she had every right to feel that way, considering what they'd done. They'd made her think about actually selling the farm, and for a while, she'd been convinced not to even go outside alone. Now, though, everything felt different. Her sister—a grown woman though she might be— needed her. They would have fun again as soon as they got through this, and Tricia *knew* she could get through it.

She took a right and hit a wall. Turning around, she went back and headed to the right again, this time finding her way around the corner. There was no good way to orient herself since even the ceiling was as dark as the midnight sky, but she could feel that they were getting through the maze. It was just an innate sense of where she was in the room, but it wasn't one that she could explain. Especially since she'd never been there before. After finding a rather hideous and brightly colored clown in the center of the maze, they threaded their way out.

"Holy hell," Tara breathed as they emerged into a huge room that'd been converted into a cemetery. "It's one thing to get a jump scare, and no one can really be expected to like spiders very much, but I don't think the people who put this place together actually thought anyone would be terrified of that. I thought I was going to have a panic attack."

"That would explain the lack of blood in my fingers," Tricia joked. "This part doesn't look so bad, though."

"Are there more zombies here?" Tara narrowed her eyes as she spotted two figures down toward the end of the room. "At least I can see them coming this time."

Tricia wasn't sure. Every other space in this haunted house had been very thematic, so she would've expected ghosts or zombies out there in the cemetery. The people ahead appeared to be children, though, and their costumes didn't exactly fit in. One was dressed as a ballerina, and the other as a cowboy. They were traditional costumes, and it was certainly a possibility that they were part of the show, but that same gut feeling that'd pulled Tricia through the maze told her that they weren't.

She had proof of that as they got closer and saw their little tear-stained faces. "Are you two okay?"

The cowboy looked up at them with big eyes and a frown. "We lost our daddy." The ballerina clung to his arm and buried her face in his plaid shirt.

"You did?" Tricia's heart might as well have been pulled out of her chest and thrown down on the fake grass under her feet. She looked around, but she didn't see anyone else nearby. "We'll help you find him."

"You will?" He picked nervously at his big belt buckle.

"Of course we will," Tara chimed in, obviously just as stricken by these poor children. "Do you think he's in here somewhere?"

The cowboy's frown deepened, and he looked as though he might start crying again. "We shouted for him, but he didn't answer."

"What if he's lost?" the ballerina asked, her voice muffled against her brother's sleeve.

"I'm sure he's not," Tricia replied, reaching out

her hand. "Why don't you two come with us? We'll find your daddy, and we won't leave you until we do."

The ballerina looked up. Her big, red-rimmed eyes looked at Tricia, then Tara, and back again. "Are you twins?"

Now that Tricia could see her face more clearly, she knew they weren't the only ones. "Yes, we are. Just like the two of you. I'm Tricia, and this is my sister Tara. Come on. Let's keep going and we'll find your dad. What's your name?"

"Mia," she sniffled.

"That's a very pretty name."

"I'm Mason," the cowboy spoke up as Tara took his hand. "I'm six."

The four of them made their way out of the cemetery and into a hallway. This time, instead of it being full of spiders, the floor was bumpy and wavy. Some places looked like giant holes were in the floor, but it was just an illusion. Tricia thought she heard a giggle from Mia as they navigated out of there and into a library where a skeleton family sat down together to read a Halloween story near the fire. There was even a skeletonized cat curled up on the hearth's rug.

"Did you like the maze?" Mason asked. "I did, but that's where we lost our dad."

"I thought the maze was scary," Tara admitted. "My sister is much braver than I am, and she had to help me get through it."

"I like this part," Mia said as she gawked at all the dusty books on the shelves, even though spider webs were stretched across them. "I like the cat."

Tricia figured it was good that they were making conversation. It meant they weren't completely scared out of their wits, as she knew she would've been if she were six years old and got separated from her parents. "Do you have any cats at home?"

"No. Daddy said we might get one someday, but not right now. He says I have to be old enough to clean the litter box and make sure I can take care of the cat all by myself." Mia adjusted her hand so that she had a better grip on Tricia's.

There was something incredibly endearing about these children, and Tricia felt a warmth radiating in her chest as they moved through the haunted house. "That sounds like a very good idea to me. What would you name a cat if you had one?"

Mia tapped her finger on her lips as she rolled her eyes up. "Pretzel."

"I like that name a lot." Tricia opened the next

door, and they were outside. Big skeletons hung from the trees, swaying slightly in the evening breeze, but the string lights and the concession stand made everything look a lot less scary.

"There's Daddy over there!" Mason exclaimed.

Tricia looked where he was pointing. A man in uniform stood talking to a zombie, gesturing emphatically toward the attraction. She thought for sure that she was looking at the wrong person because it was unmistakably Duke. When Mason and Mia let go of Tara and Tricia's hands to run over and wrap their arms around his legs, however, she knew he was the right person.

"There you are! Oh, thank god!" Duke bent forward and put his hands on their backs. "I was just about to have them shut the whole place down until we found you. How did you get out?"

"We met these nice ladies." Mason gestured toward them.

Feeling her cheeks warm up as they always did when she was around the gorgeous police chief, Tricia gave a finger wave. "Hi, Duke."

The shock on his handsome face was just as price-less as the joy on his kids' faces at being reunited with their dad. His gaze locked on hers, those deep blue eyes simmering with warmth and desire. "Tricia. Hi. It's nice to see you again. And um, thank you. We went through that maze, and then they were just gone."

Tricia shrugged. She would've helped Mason and Mia no matter whose children they were, but it was certainly an interesting twist of fate that they belonged to Duke. "It happens. It wasn't a problem."

"Kids." Duke turned around to gesture at a slightly older boy, who'd been hanging back a little. "I guess I should officially introduce you to our new neighbor, Tricia. And this is her sister, Tara. You already know Mason and Mia, and this is my older son, Oliver."

Mia grinned up at Tricia before she turned back to her father. "She's just as pretty as you said, Daddy."

Now it was time for Duke's face to get red, and he swiped a hand through his hair. He shrugged a little in apology.

"I'm hungry," Mason said, wistfully looking at the concession stand.

"Me, too," Oliver agreed.

"Of course." Still a bit rattled, he patted his pockets until he found his wallet. "I need to take care of this. Tricia, if you could wait for just a moment, I'd like to speak with you."

"You go ahead," Tara volunteered, moving toward the children. "I'll get their food for them."

Duke instantly held out his debit card. "Anything they want."

Tricia stepped aside with Duke, moving out of the way of the people exiting the haunted house but still within a clear line of sight of his children. "I'm surprised you'd just hand your debit card over to someone who's practically a complete stranger."

"I don't think I can call her a stranger when she and her sister just rescued my children for me. Plus, she'd be pretty bold if she was going to blatantly rip off the chief of police." He pulled in a deep breath and let it out slowly, still trying to calm himself. "Besides, I don't exactly consider you a stranger."

She smiled at that, even though she wasn't quite sure what the two of them were. Not strangers, no. Friends? Neighbors? Something more? It was hard to say, but she wasn't going to ask him. "I suppose not. Are you all right? I know that had to be hard."

"I'm fine, or at least I will be. It all worked out. There are a lot of terrifying moments when you have children." He watched them as they discussed the menu with Tara.

"I suppose that's true," Tricia murmured. Not that she would know herself or that she ever even wanted to know. It always looked like an awful lot of work, and the way Duke's blood had drained from his face when he couldn't find his kids was proof of it.

"That's been handled, but there's something else I need to take care of." He was standing a little straighter now, more confident and focused. He was returning to the Duke she'd known, the one who confidently strutted naked in front of his bathroom window and carried her out of a field. "Would you have dinner with me sometime?"

Her heart surged toward him. She'd thought of him every day since she'd arrived in Carlton, and the fact that she kept running into him one way or another only increased the frequency. But Duke was vulnerable right now, even if his machismo wouldn't let him show it. Having dinner with him sounded wonderful in theory, but she was starting to think she'd been hoping for too much when it came to Duke. "You don't have to do that."

Seeing that Tara and the kids were doing just fine and weren't going anywhere, Duke turned to her fully. "What do you mean?"

"You don't owe me anything for helping your

kids. Even if you did, I'd say we're about even considering that you took me to the hospital." In fact, he was ahead of her in that regard. He'd not only gotten her out of the field and to the hospital, but he'd stayed far longer than he'd had to. Duke would've been fully justified in getting her to the ER and then going about his business, but that wasn't what he'd done.

He moved closer, close enough that it would take only the smallest movement to be in each other's arms. "This isn't about being even."

Tricia's breath froze in her lungs, and her stomach ignited with energy. Sparks radiated through her body as she felt the potential between them, a tightness that built with every encounter, promising at some point to explode. Duke had a magnetic quality about him, and all the logic she'd tried to use on herself was suddenly no longer valid. "I suppose it's not," she replied breathlessly, surprised she could get the words out, considering the riot happening within her body.

"So you'll go with me?" he pressed.

How could she say no? It didn't truly matter because she didn't want to say no. Tricia took a deep breath, but the expansion of her lungs brought the two of them that much closer together. "Yes, I will."

"Tomorrow night, then. I'll pick you up at eight. And don't worry. I've already got your address." With one last smoldering look, he turned to join his children at one of the picnic tables, where they were just getting seated with corn dogs, candy apples, and big cups of cider.

12

Duke knotted his tie and grimaced into the mirror. Several shirts and pants lay behind him on the bed, each having only been tried on for a minute or two. He'd even put some of them on twice, but nothing seemed quite right. He didn't like how his shoes looked with one pair of pants, or a shirt was too scratchy, and another was too loud. Sighing, he turned and stomped out into the hallway.

The smell of chili enticed him into the kitchen. "Are you trying to make me change my mind about going out tonight?"

Emily smiled as she lifted the lid off the pot and gave it a stir. She held her nose over the concoction for a moment before she tossed in another handful of chipotle powder. "Certainly not, considering it's the first time you've gone anywhere but work or the grocery store in months. Maybe even longer. It's about time." The older woman replaced the lid and set her big wooden spoon on a small rest nearby.

"I guess it is," he admitted. There had been little reason for him to go anywhere for a while. He was needed at work, and he was definitely needed at home. He knew how much time Emily had invested into his family, so he'd had difficulty asking her to stay that evening. She'd seemed pleased at the idea, but he still found doubts creeping into the back of his mind. What if Mia had a nightmare? What if Mason and Oliver climbed up on the roof to see if they could fly? Some of that was extreme, but he'd certainly learned that things could change quickly. He'd hate to be gone if it turned out he was needed there.

Bracing one hand on the counter, Emily gave him that motherly look of hers. "What's on your mind?"

"I'm just having a hard time deciding on an outfit. How's this?" Duke held his arms wide. He wasn't exactly one for fashion, which was probably a good thing since he usually wore a uniform. Hell, wearing that uniform all the time might be exactly why he wasn't one for fashion. There was no need to

pay attention to trends when you grabbed a dupli-
cate copy of yesterday's outfit out of the closet most
days of the week.

Emily tipped her head to the side, considering.
"That depends. Where are you taking her?"

"I don't believe I mentioned anything about a
woman," Duke noted.

"Do you really think you can fool me? You've
shaved, and your shoes are buffed. You're either
going to court, or a woman is waiting for you."

"If we get an opening for a detective, you'll be the
first person I call. We're going to The Crimson Lily."
It was the nicest restaurant in town, and Duke
worried it might be too nice. It wasn't like he was
proposing to her or anything. On the other hand,
something too casual wouldn't really seem like a
date. His father had always said it was better to be
overdressed than underdressed, and Duke figured
the same logic could apply to the restaurant.

"Very nice," Emily said approvingly as she took
in his black button-down and gray trousers. "I think
you'll look absolutely perfect if you just go put a
belt on."

"Right." Duke wondered how he could forget
something so simple. "Of course. I'll do that."

Just then, the twins came storming in from the

backyard. Their cheeks were pink from the cool weather, and their eyes were bright. "We raked up a big pile of leaves!" Mason enthused. "Then we jumped in it."

"Good for you," Duke said with a laugh as he pulled a leaf out of Mia's hair. "It looks like you might have to bring the rake in here, judging by your clothes."

"We're going back out after we get a drink," Mia advised, as if that made a difference on just how much of the yard they were tracking in.

"I'll get you some juice." Emily was already opening the fridge.

"I'll have some, too, please," Oliver said as he stepped in from the living room.

Mason paused as he looked at his father. "Where are you going?"

Oh, boy. This was the part he'd been dreading. There was a little embarrassment when it came to telling Emily, but telling the kids was much more difficult. There would be so many questions, and they might even be upset. That would make it even harder for him to leave, but that was exactly why he'd gotten ready early. There wasn't any point in hiding it from them. That wasn't the sort of father he was. "I'm taking Tricia out to dinner."

"Eww, you have a date?" Mason asked.   He backed away, holding his hands up in front of him. "You'd better not touch me when you get back.   I don't want your cooties!"

"I didn't even know cooties were still a thing," Duke noted quietly.

Emily simply shrugged.

"Are you going to kiss her?" Mia asked.

Duke opened his mouth and then shut it again. He'd certainly like to kiss Tricia–and plenty more if he were honest–but that was one thing he couldn't discuss with his children. "Well, um..."

"Eww! Then you'll have a *lot* of cooties!" Mason squealed. He pursed his lips to make kissing noises, and his sister joined in. Soon enough, the kissing sounds descended into pure giggles.

"All right, that's enough of that. You two take these outside."   Emily handed them their cups of juice and opened the back door.

Duke could see them run to the patio table with their cups in hand, still laughing. Oliver had left as well, returning to whatever he was watching on TV. "I guess I don't have to worry about them."

"No, I'd say not. And even once they settle down, I've got plenty to keep them occupied. I brought over some of my kids' favorite Halloween movies—

nothing too scary—and we'll have some snacks."
Emily smiled, pleased with herself.

Duke had to admit he was pretty pleased, as
well. The kids didn't seem bothered in the least by
him going out with Tricia. Granted, that was probably because they'd already had a chance to meet
her, and she and Tara had 'rescued' them from the
haunted house. If this actually went anywhere—
Duke reminded himself that was a big *if*—it was
starting off on good footing. He headed back to his
bedroom, knowing he couldn't even feel guilty about
asking Emily to put some extra hours in since she
seemed so delighted to be doing so.

He took one last look in the mirror. Emily said
the outfit was fine, so it would just have to be good
enough. Duke took his wallet and keys from the
nightstand and felt his stomach lurch. This was
more real than stopping by to introduce himself to a
new neighbor or running into her at a party. In a
way, it was even bigger than finding her in the field.
That'd been an urgent matter, and he'd felt things he
never expected to feel for a woman again, but it was
still an accident. Dinner was planned. It was time
that they'd specifically set aside for each other
instead of waiting for fate to intervene once again.

Duke was so lost in thought that he almost didn't

hear the soft knock on his door. Oliver poked his head in. "Dad?"

"Hey, son. Come on in." Duke patted his pockets, feeling like he was forgetting something.

Oliver sat down on the corner of the mattress and stared down at his hands. "I guess you must really like Tricia."

His worries instantly came flooding back. Mason and Mia clearly didn't care, but they were younger. They were more interested in seeing how many beetles they could catch in the backyard or heading into town for ice cream. Oliver was a harder nut to crack, and he'd also been much more closed off since Lynne died.

Duke sat down on the bed next to him. "What makes you say that?"

Oliver shrugged, but when Duke gave him a few more seconds of silence, he finally pointed to the dresser. "You're wearing your special cologne, the one you only used to wear when you and Mom were going out on a date."

"I see." And he did. Duke's eyes landed on that bottle of cologne. It was expensive, the kind of thing he'd never splurge on for himself. He'd tried it in a department store in Portland, and Lynne had gone back and bought it for him for Christmas. He'd used it sparingly, knowing he'd never buy himself another bottle.

That meant he hadn't used it in a year, yet Oliver remembered the scent well. "Does that bother you?"

He shrugged again, and his lips pursed slightly. "I don't know. Do you like Tricia?"

"I do." But it wasn't as simple as that, and Duke knew it. The complexities that came with attraction and interest were hard to talk about, even with other adults. Oliver was uncertain about this whole thing, but the truth was that Duke felt the same way. "Right now, though, we're just going out for dinner. We're going to spend some time together and get to know each other a little more."

Oliver's feet were bare, and he scrunched his toes into the carpet. "So it's not, like, you're getting married or anything?"

Oh, god. Duke put his arm around his son and rested his cheek against his sandy brown hair, hair that was the same color as Lynne's. "Is that something you worry about?"

"Not really. Well, I didn't. But then Noah told me about how his parents divorced, and his dad married this other woman. Now his dad is always off doing other things with his new wife and her kids, and Noah hardly ever sees him anymore." Oliver's skinny shoulders hunched up toward his ears. "It sounds like it kind of sucks."

"Yeah, it does," Duke agreed. "I think a lot of people have a hard time figuring out how to deal with their family after a death or divorce. Sometimes they don't make the right choices, or even if they do, they don't always look like the right choices to everyone else."

"I guess." Oliver didn't seem convinced.

Duke pulled back so he could look Oliver in the face. "The most important thing we have going for our family is that you kids are at the top of my list. I'm always looking out for you, whether I'm seeing anyone or not. If I get to the point where I think I might want to be married again, she'll have to be really special. She'll be someone we all care about because I wouldn't want to be with someone who wouldn't treasure you as much as I do."

Oliver put his arms around Duke's chest and hugged him tightly, and Duke hugged him right back. He knew his son's squeeze would put wrinkles in his shirt, but he didn't care. That just meant he'd be carrying Oliver's love with him for the rest of the night. They sat like that for several minutes, just holding each other.

"Is there anything else you want to talk about?" Duke asked when Oliver pulled back.

"No, I guess not." He still looked a little down, but he wasn't nearly as upset as he'd been when he first arrived. Oliver rubbed his hands together. "Tricia does seem nice."

"You think so? I didn't think you really got to speak with her at all yesterday." Not that he was arguing. If he had the approval of all three of his kids and Emily, he'd feel much better about heading out the door.

Another shrug, and then Oliver looked off to the left. "I don't know. She just... seems nice."

Duke knew he was hiding something. That look had been Oliver's tell ever since he was little, but Duke knew better than to call him out on it. "If you want to talk more, just let me know."

"Okay." Oliver got up, and he paused when he reached the door. "Will you come in and let me know when you're home?"

It would be late, well past his bedtime. "Of course."

13

Tricia smiled as Duke held out her chair for her, waiting until she was seated before he went around to his side of the table. Their date had just barely started, and already he'd been a perfect gentleman. He'd insisted on opening her car door both to let her in and out, and then, of course, he'd opened the door to the restaurant. The final touch was the way his fingers grazed the small of her back as she walked in through the door of The Crimson Lily.

She tried to remind herself that lots of men did that when things were fresh and new, and they were still trying to make a good impression. That didn't mean it lasted or that a guy was as good as he was pretending to be. On the backside of that thought, she chided herself for being so jaded. If Duke had been sweet so far, couldn't she just appreciate that?

"This is a nice place," she said as she looked around. The décor was elegant and sleek, with black walls contrasting the bright white tablecloths. Potted plants were dotted around the dining area, lending just enough softness to break up the sharpness of the rest of the room, but there weren't so many that they got in the way. Bolts of red broke through the décor here and there in the napkins, candles, and menus.

Duke had cleaned up rather nicely, and that soft desire in his eyes didn't hurt. "They have excellent food and good service."

As if to prove his point, a waiter appeared at their table immediately and requested their drink orders.

Tricia's stomach had been jumpy all day, so she ordered a glass of wine to calm her nerves. It seemed that there was something inevitable between the two of them, and neither had the power to resist it any longer. She hadn't been able to decide if that was a good or bad thing.

"How is your arm?" Duke asked as he focused in on her cast.

She frowned down at it but made herself smile when she looked back up. He'd seemed so concerned, almost acting as though the injury had been his fault. "It's a little difficult to find a nice outfit that still works with a big cast on my arm, but otherwise, it seems to be doing well. It doesn't hurt much, and Tara has been coming over to help me with the things I can't do on my own right now."

"You look just fine to me."

This made Tricia look down again at the outfit she'd finally settled on. The simple black dress was an easy choice, but figuring out how to dress it up or down hadn't been. Her broken arm really had dictated things in the end because the champagne knee-length cardigan had loose sleeves that came down just to the top of the cast. A long necklace and tall boots had finished up the ensemble, and she felt much better about it now that she could see how he was dressed. "Thank you."

"I'm right next door, you know," he reminded her, "if there's something that you need or your sister's busy." Those midnight eyes blazed into hers.

Tricia knew that if Duke had come over to help her wash her hair, she might not actually have gotten clean at all. "That's kind of you. So far, I've been managing. I have to admit, though, I still can't figure out why this Charlie Johnston guy is so hung up on the land."

Duke leaned forward. "He hasn't bothered you anymore, has he?"

"No," she replied quickly, seeing that he was concerned. Did he care simply because he was the chief of police and it was his job to keep Carlton's citizens safe or was it something else? "I haven't seen him at all since, but I'm still trying to wrap my head around what would make someone go to such extremes just for a remote piece of farmland and a little old house."

Their drinks arrived just then, but since they hadn't even opened their menus, Duke sent him away for the moment.

Duke took a sip of his tea and braced his fore-arms on the table, looking like he was trying to figure out how to say something. "Fiona's husband was a Johnston. I take it you weren't particularly close to his family?"

She let out a bit of a laugh. "Or even to him, honestly. When we came to visit, we were always there for Fiona. Dick was always in town at the bar or off with his buddies. Tara and I never knew him all that well, and we were content to leave it that way."

He nodded, his forehead creasing a little. "You could say there's a bit of a feud between the Johnstons and another large family around here, the Thompsons."

"I've seen the name around quite a bit." Her wine wasn't from Cloud Ridge, but it was damn good. Tricia made a mental note to figure out what it was so she could report back to Tara. "I didn't realize feuds were still a thing."

"It's a little more subtle than what you see in the movies or the cartoons. Both the Johnstons and Thompsons have been logging families for generations. A lot of their disputes arise from timber rights or contracts on certain lands. It's been going on for far longer than that, though, and it wasn't always about business. A lot of the details are fuzzy for me, but I guess there was an engagement that got broken off."

"Right. When Beatrice Thompson refused to marry Harold Johnston," Tricia filled in.

The look of shock on Duke's face was priceless. "How do you know that? I didn't even know their names."

She lifted a shoulder and then winced when she

realized it was the wrong one. "I found a box of old letters in the attic," Tricia explained, eager to get Duke's attention back on the story and off of her arm. The way he worried over it made something twist inside her guts, something that also made her wish they didn't have this table between them. "I guess Fiona had kept them, although they had to be from even before her time. They're from a few different people in both families, and all are addressed to Dorothy Johnston. It's been a little hard to piece together, but it sounds like Beatrice and Harold were supposed to get married. Beatrice broke off the engagement, and the Johnstons were furious."

"That's because both of the families were rich and powerful, at least for the times. The Johnstons thought they could have it all if a Thompson married in and her property got transferred to them. It's a real shame, though." He shook his head as he studied the flickering candle flame for a moment.

"Why?" Tricia asked. "It sounds like Beatrice wouldn't marry Harold because she found a man she truly loved. How did she put it? 'Warren and I are fated to each other. Destiny put him in my way to save me from an uncertain future, uncertain in every sense except for the guarantee that I would be unhappy.' I thought it was kind of romantic. She found her true love just in time, right before entering what sounds like an arranged marriage."

Duke lifted his eyes to hers, and there was an incredible sadness in them. "It's a shame because Beatrice was murdered. She was found with a young man named Warren Rodgers, but the newspapers at the time could only speculate as to what their relationship was. I guess the families were too ashamed of her running off with him that they never revealed it to the press."

Her heart sank in her chest, and a chill ran up her spine. "That's horrible. Did the Johnstons have her killed?"

"It would seem so."

"Oh." Tricia sagged back in her seat. It was no wonder Duke had freaked out when she'd told him about her encounters with Charlie Johnston, and she couldn't really blame him for not wanting her to be outside by herself. Granted, the people they were discussing had been dead for a long time, but it was clear that some of that hateful vengeance still existed in the Johnston bloodline.

"I'm sorry. I shouldn't have even brought that up."

Duke reached across the table and touched the back of her hand. "Since you've apparently decided you're not going to let the Johnstons get that land out from under you, why don't you tell me about your plans for it? Are you going to be a full-time pumpkin farmer?"

She didn't know if he was truly interested or just making small talk to lighten the mood, but Tricia found that she enjoyed discussing her future with the property. It seemed full of possibilities, even if none of them could happen right away. "As full-time as I can be, anyway. I still have a lot to learn, but I suppose I have all winter for that. I thought it'd be nice to at least open to the public as a simple pumpkin patch this year. Next year, it'd be great to really expand the place. The front yard has some perfect spots for photo ops, with those painted props with cutouts that kids can put their faces in, or benches with corn stalks and hay bales all around. I also found a great idea online for a jack-o-lantern-themed beanbag toss that looked like it'd be easy to put together." Tricia fiddled with the chain of her necklace as she lost herself in all the ideas she'd been gathering.

"It sounds great," Duke enthused. "I think the town would go nuts for it, and so would my kids.

They've had a hard time over the past year, and I've tried to keep them distracted when I can."

Tricia picked up her menu, realizing the waiter had breezed by a few times to check on them. "Since you and their mother split up, I'm assuming."

"Actually, no. She passed away."

Horror prickled over her skin as she looked over the top of the menu, and the small amount of wine in her stomach threatened to come back up. "I'm so sorry. I didn't realize..."

"No, no. It's okay," he assured her. "It's just one of those things. You don't really want to talk about it, but you can't avoid it altogether. I've had to accept that it's just part of who I am now. We all have our stories that we bring along with us."

She swallowed, grateful when the waiter stopped by and placed a basket of bread on the table. Tricia had to get something in her stomach. "I suppose that's true."

Duke had that blazing look again, the one that made her feel as though he'd only have to ask, and she'd bare her soul to him. "What about you?"

Tricia's throat tried to reject the nibble of bread, but she forced it down before she choked on it. "What about me?"

"Why are you single?" he asked with a smile.

"We might as well get it all out in the open, especially since we've managed to avoid all these conversations until now. How is it that some man hasn't snagged you up and kept you for his own?"

It was supposed to be lighthearted and flattering, and Tricia did her best to shift herself in that direction as well. "It's not always easy to find the right person. You don't usually find them in a bar, and since I was a hairdresser back in Eugene, I didn't meet many guys at work. There are tons of dating sites and apps these days, but you just never know who you're going to meet."

"You might even find a guy who towels off with his curtains open," Duke joked.

Tricia laughed at that, and in an instant, the chemistry she always felt with him came roaring back to life. She had to give him credit for being willing to bring it up. "Exactly! There was this one guy who was completely obsessed with serial killers."

"A lot of people are if the shows on Netflix are anything to gauge it by," Duke reasoned.

"Right? The guy was also a teacher, and every time I talked to him, he basically assigned me homework on a serial killer to look up so we could discuss him the next time. It was a little much." The guy had also tried to kiss her at the end of their date, which she'd found so repulsive, she'd practically run away. Considering what she and Duke had already done *without* an official date, she thought that part was better left unsaid.

Duke laughed. "They can't all be *that* bad."

"Maybe not, but there are other little things. I never thought people had to have every single thing in common to be compatible, but a person's general lifestyle is still important." She tipped her head back as she remembered some of the guys who'd seemed interesting at first but quickly showed it would never work out. "I don't necessarily want to move to Alaska or join a certain church to be with someone. Or plenty of people want to have children. You can't really skirt around those issues and still have a successful relationship."

"You don't want children?" Something had changed in Duke's eyes.

Tricia felt that chemistry fade into the background again, but this time it wasn't just a shift in mood. This was something much deeper. She felt him pull back from her, even though he hadn't moved an inch physically. "It's a really big commitment, the kind of thing I was never sure about. The sleepless nights, the expense, the complete dedication of your life. I know a lot of people think it's the best thing that's happened to them, but after seeing everything my sister went through with her kids, I decided it just wasn't for me."

"That's understandable." Duke picked up his menu. "The filet mignon is supposed to be phenomenal here."

She dropped her eyes back down to her own menu, but Tricia could hardly even see the words. What had made her think this would be different from any other time with any other man?

It was that knight in shining armor bullshit, probably. She'd let herself think it was more than just him doing his job. Who the hell *wouldn't* pick their neighbor up out of a field and take them to the hospital? It would've said a lot more about him if he hadn't than the fact that he had.

Combined with the hot and heavy sex they'd had up against the brewery, Tricia had fooled herself into believing this wasn't like what she'd experienced with dating apps. She'd let herself think this was real and, somehow, more pure. But when it boiled right down to the facts, to those important things that couldn't be avoided, he just was another guy who wouldn't work out.

Sadness washed over her. Just like anyone else,

she wanted someone to belong with. She wanted to find a person she was fated to be with, as Beatrice Thompson had put it. Granted, she'd had to pay the ultimate price for finding her love. Tricia wondered if, as she died, Beatrice had thought it was all still worth it.

14

"HEY. ARE YOU ALL RIGHT?"

Duke looked up at the sharp elbow in the ribs he'd just received from August. "Yeah, I'm fine."

The old dragon's eyes looked at him with concern. "Are you sure? You look like me when I've been down at the station too much, and it's time to get a well-deserved vacation in." August Hill was the fire chief in Carlton, and he could certainly relate.

"Sure. It must be something like that." Duke rubbed his hand over his eyes, wishing it was that simple. Other than that episode in the grocery store parking lot, the radios had been fairly quiet. A few fender benders and a burning bag of dog poop on someone's front step weren't enough to keep him distracted from his personal problems.

August gave him a smile that was a bit too wide for his face. "You know, you've got a competent crew working under you. They can handle things if you need to get away for a bit. It feels strange to accept that they can get along without you, but that just means you're doing your job right."

"I'll keep it in mind," Duke promised him. Getting away from Carlton would be a welcomed reprieve, but he couldn't just leave his kids to celebrate Halloween alone while he ran off to a beach somewhere. And if he brought them along, they'd be missing school.

Then there was Tricia. Duke shifted in his chair, trying to pay attention to the clan meeting. As one of the community leaders of Carlton, he needed to know what was going on in town. Somehow, he'd been able to talk to her about the Thompsons as though they were a completely separate family. His last name might be different, but on his mother's side, he was just as much a Thompson as any other bear in the room.

It hadn't just been the depressing downturn in their conversation about the clan disputes that'd ruined his date with Tricia. It hadn't even been that he'd had to bring up Lynne. He didn't regret that because anyone who had a chance to be part of his life would need to know. But her revelation about not wanting children had cut him like a cold knife, a blow so hard he was surprised he hadn't fallen over.

Tricia simultaneously threw his bear into a protective rage and a demanding fervor. It was desperate to be near her, constantly reminding Duke of how it felt when a shifter found the other half of their soul. That'd been hard to deal with, considering Lynne had made him feel the same way. After fate had shoved them together so many times, though, he'd decided he'd just have to get past whatever hang-ups he had about finding a second true love.

But then to hear that she didn't want children? How the hell was he supposed to deal with that? He already had three of them. Duke couldn't just make them go away, nor would he want to. He'd told them a thousand times that they were his world and his heart, and he'd meant every word. Tricia had been the first person he'd even been willing to go out to dinner with. Plenty of other women in town had certainly tried once they knew he was single. It was downright cruel for destiny to dangle Tricia in front of him like that and then snatch her away.

He glanced around the meeting. The clanhouse was particularly full that day. Duke had to wonder if any of them had felt the same heartache he now suffered with.

Chris Thompson flipped the page on his meeting notes. "The last thing I'd like to remind you about before we go is that we're coming up on the holiday season. I know it's not Halloween quite yet, but before we know it, the weather will be turning colder. I ask you all to do as we've always done. Check in on your friends and neighbors, particularly those who are older or who have other struggles. We're a large clan, and our members have many talents. We've been able to give food and shelter to those who need it when times get hard, and that's always at the top of my agenda. This is a reminder that you don't have to wait until an official meeting to bring up someone in need, nor do you have to make it public if you'd rather not. My door is always open. I think that takes care of everything for tonight." The Alpha picked up his notes and tapped them into a neat stack to signify that he was done.

Duke watched as the members stood up. They stretched and chatted with each other as they slowly put on their jackets or made their way to the door. Some stopped to grab one of the few pumpkin spice cookies that remained on a long side table, courtesy of Brandy. They were carrying on with their lives, living as though they didn't have an ache so deep in their hearts that it was almost impossible to stand. Did he look that way on the surface? Judging by the way August had been talking to him, probably not.

He moved up to the front of the room, where Chris was chatting with an older woman. "I think that would be a great idea. We'll discuss it a little more and get back to you."

"Thank you, dear." The woman moved off, stopping at the table for a cookie.

"You guys have a moment to chat?" Duke asked. "In private."

Chris wrinkled one dark auburn eyebrow in curiosity, but he nodded. "We can always spare a moment for the police chief." He led the way into the hall and through a door.

Duke knew he was doing the right thing but didn't like it. It was his job for people to come to him with problems and for him to fix them. Not the other way around. Still, the Alpha and beta of the Thompson clan had a lot of resources at their disposal, not to mention generations of experience. Chris, his father, and his grandfather had all done a good job of leading this clan, and Duke knew he had to respect that.

Tyler closed the door behind them. "If this is about that speeding ticket that Liz got last week, she's going to get that taken care of. She was trying to get to one of her reiki patients who was in a lot of pain, and she wasn't really paying attention to the speed limit."

"No, it's not about that," Duke replied. He'd noticed Liz's ticket come across, but he hadn't been all that concerned about it. "I actually have some interesting news from the border."

The two brothers shared a glance. "That's unusual," Chris commented as he took a seat behind his big desk and leaned back in his chair. "We haven't heard anything about that being an issue for quite some time."

Guilt washed over Duke. Once again, he saw an injured Tricia in his mind's eye, with pumpkin debris in her hair and dirt all over her clothes. If he'd done a better job, that might not have happened at all. Even so, nothing he did would be good enough to change things between them. Duke cleared his throat, trying to stay centered on the clan matter at hand, not the matter of his heart. "For the most part, it hasn't been. I'm here about the farm that sits just west of me, the one that had belonged to Dick and Fiona Johnston."

It was a parcel of land that both men knew about, considering the property line between Duke's house and Fiona's farm was essentially the very border he was supposed to be keeping an eye on. "I heard she passed it on to a family member," Tyler noted.

"Yes," Duke affirmed. "Her niece, Tricia Fitzpatrick, who happens to be a human."

Chris steepled his fingers under his chin. "Mmm. That could be complicated. Should I assume that she already knows about shifters if she's in the family?"

"I don't believe she does." He couldn't be sure, of course. Duke hadn't dared to bring up such a thing in front of Tricia. If she'd known, though, she would've already understood just how clan dynamics worked and that the 'feud' between them wasn't a simple matter of who had which last name.

"Is this woman a threat in some way?" Tyler asked.

"No." A threat to his heart, to his mental well-being, and to whether or not he could keep his bear in check, yes. But not to the clan. "The problem is that the Johnstons are threatening her. She owns the land now, but she's just a human as far as they're concerned. We all know how the Johnstons feel about them."

Both of the Thompson men nodded. This was something they'd had to deal with on more than one occasion.

"Charlie Johnston paid her a visit, offering to buy the land from her. She refused, knowing only that they were distant cousins of hers by marriage. Then he came back, and when she still wouldn't sell, one of his delinquents pushed her. She ended up breaking her arm." Would he ever be able to think about that day without his gut twisting? Tricia was fine now, and there was no need for him to still have that reaction.

Chris braced his hand on his chin. "A cowardly move on his part, but not one that surprises me in the least. Has she heard any more from Charlie?"

"No." Or at least if she had, she hadn't told Duke about it. Now that this gap had opened between them, he had to wonder just how much Tricia would be willing to tell him. He needed to be kept apprised if he was going to help, but Tricia likely didn't know just how much danger she was in. "I understand that he hasn't said anything else, but I don't trust him. I'm sure Tricia doesn't realize that her property is right on the edge of some very dangerous territory."

Putting his hands behind his head, Chris looked at his brother. "I guess that explains why we didn't have any real issues with the Johnstons on the agenda for this meeting. Fred was letting his nephew cause trouble in a more subtle way than usual."

Though it didn't necessarily have anything to do with him or this scenario, Duke couldn't help but think of what'd happened to Beatrice Thompson and Warren Rodgers. It proved to him that the Johnstons had always been willing to go out of their way to get what they wanted, and they didn't care who had to pay the price for it. "I had a few words with Charlie recently at the scene of an accident, but I'm still concerned that this might escalate. It's clear that the Johnstons want that property back, and they obviously think they'll be able to coerce her into it because she's human."

Tyler rubbed a hand through his short dark hair. "It sounds to me like we need to have an extra shift or two on watch. You can't be there all the time, but you know you've always got the full support of the clan behind you. Don't worry about feeling like you have to host anyone, either. We can station them out in the woods, and no one will know they're there unless there's trouble."

Chris nodded his agreement. "This could be a good chance to try the dedicated emergency number we've been talking about. I want a guaranteed way for our members to get a hold of someone. It's not always practical to shift and reach out telepathically. Then, of course, there's the risk that those available wouldn't be in their bear form."

"Like 911 for the clan," Duke concluded.

"Exactly," Tyler affirmed. "I've already been talking with someone at Taylor Communications, and the technology is already easily available. I'll get it set up right away, and then you can get us with the push of a button."

That was enough to ease a bit of the tension Duke held in his muscles, but it wouldn't take care of everything. "Thank you. I'll let you know if I find out anything else."

"That would be good," Chris agreed. "It doesn't bother me at all if that property is in neutral hands, but the more ground the Johnstons gain, the more confident they're going to get. I'll make sure everyone knows to be on alert in case you need assistance."

"Thank you again. I'll leave you to the rest of

your night." Duke made his way upstairs and out the front door to his car.

He'd talked with his clan leaders, and that should've made him feel infinitely better about the situation. Everyone knew what was happening, and he would have someone nearby if the Johnstons decided to push this further. Knowing Chris, he would probably even attempt to have a meeting with Fred Johnston and see if they could nip the issue in the bud. Not that Duke had any confidence in Fred being cooperative, but Chris would do whatever he could to take care of this diplomatically. That was one of the many reasons he was a great Alpha.

For Duke, though, the opposing clan was only part of the problem. He wanted Tricia, and not just for a few lusty minutes at a party. It wasn't mere desire, although she was certainly attractive enough. It was the way she tugged on his very soul, a constant reminder of what could be between them.

Except that it couldn't. She'd made that very clear at dinner the night before. Duke didn't doubt that she found him attractive. Why else would she look at him like that, with her fingers unconsciously touching her hair or lingering near her neckline? Why else would her face light up every time she looked at him? Despite all of that, Duke had some-thing she didn't want.

His bear was just going to have to learn to live with that. Mia, Mason, and Oliver were his life, and nothing would change that.

15

THE SUN WAS ON HER SHOULDERS, AND A BREEZE ruffled through her hair. It was a beautiful day to be outside, and the pumpkin patch held the entirety of Tricia's focus. As she'd been telling Tara all along, she wouldn't be able to get much done that year. That didn't mean she wasn't going to give it her all. The place deserved it, and she had a feeling Fiona would be proud to see her out there working the field, broken arm and all.

Of course, that broken arm was making things rather difficult. The mini pumpkins were easy enough to load into the wheelbarrow and take up to the front of the property, where she'd arranged them in an old wooden crate. Now she was working on the pie pumpkins, which were already proving to be much more awkward than the little ones. Tricia knew that pumpkins shouldn't be picked up by the stem, which didn't leave her a lot of options. She scooped her hand underneath one, balancing it against her palm and wrist as she slowly transferred it into the wheelbarrow.

"I'm going to need to get a tractor at some point," she mumbled, laughing a little as she envisioned herself behind the wheel of a big John Deere, hauling a homemade cart full of pumpkins from the back acreage. If her salon clients back in Eugene could only see her now.

As she worked, she made a point not to look over at Duke's house. That was a tactic she'd tried before, but this time, she was determined to follow through with it. She'd been excited about going out with him, but their date had been nothing short of awkward. A feud that'd ended in murder? The death of his wife and the subsequent distress of his children? The last straw was discovering that the two of them had some major foundational differences.

The worst part was that she should've seen it coming. She stood up straight and pulled the wheelbarrow with her as she moved to the next area of the field. Duke hadn't told her about his children right away, nor had he had a reason to. But she'd certainly known about them when she'd agreed to dinner. She'd even been holding Mia's hand! So why hadn't she let that stop her from saying yes? Why had she led both herself and Duke on by entertaining the idea of a date?

She'd let herself be dazzled by his good looks and gallantry. He seemed to be a truly good man, a rare thing these days. It made it easy enough for her to overlook everything else.

Wiping a bit of sweat off her brow with the back of her sleeve, Tricia had to admit that his children had been awfully sweet. She'd seen that scared look in their eyes, and her heart had instantly reached out toward them. That was even before she'd known who their father was. Tricia couldn't deny that there'd been an instant attachment there.

Still, he was a man who was committed to his children, as he should be. She was different, someone who lived her own life. Neither one of them could change that.

Her good wrist started to ache as she reached for the next pumpkin. The work was only getting harder, and she was exhausting herself. Tricia realized she just might have to let customers come pick their own pumpkins after all since she couldn't seem to get the job done. As she struggled to get a grip on the squash, a pair of small hands appeared on either side of it and lifted it right up off the ground.

"I've got it."

Startled, Tricia looked up to see a set of familiar blue eyes. "Mia? What are you doing here?"

She put the pumpkin in the cart with the others. "We came outside to play, and we wanted to help."

"Oh. How very sweet of you." Tricia looked around to find that 'we' included Mason and Oliver, who were coming up behind their sister. "I'm just trying to get some of these picked and put out front so I can sell them."

"I've got this one!" Mason jumped in to assist, plucking a fat orange globe from the ground and adding it to the others.

"I want to get the big ones," Oliver said, gesturing with his hands to show the size of the carving pumpkins. "Do you have another wheelbarrow?"

"I'm sorry. I just have this one." Tricia felt lame admitting that, realizing perhaps she'd been doing everything the hard way and a nine-year-old boy might have better ideas than she did.

But he wasn't the only one who was a good problem-solver. "I'll get my wagon!" Mia announced, running back off toward their property.

By the time she returned, Mason had already filled Tricia's wheelbarrow with pie pumpkins. "Where do you want these?" He got in front of it and hefted the handles, clearly ready to take it wherever she asked him to.

It was the sweetest thing she'd ever seen. "Wouldn't you kids rather be playing? Not that I don't appreciate your help, but I don't want to take up your time."

Mason looked at his sister and then his brother. Some sort of communication must've passed between them because he shrugged his shoulders. "Nah."

Who was she to turn down those bright, eager faces? "Okay. Well, I want to put them right up here. I had someone load a couple of bales of straw into my trunk, and I was going to use those as a little display. I haven't gotten them out yet, though, so we can put the pumpkins on the ground for the moment."

"I can help you with it," Mason insisted.

"Are you sure? They're probably heavy." Tricia was starting to feel guilty about letting them do so much.

"Yeah. Dad and I put straw out in the yard every year to keep it from getting too muddy," he insisted.

The worst that could happen was not being able to get the straw bales out of the trunk, and Tricia would have to leave them there for a little longer. Duke had said he would help her with anything she needed, but she knew she couldn't ask him. Not after that dinner.

Fortunately, Mason proved to be just as much help as he'd said he'd be. "You hold the string on that end, and I'll get this end," he directed. "Hold both strings so one doesn't slip off."

The straw was lighter than she'd imagined, even with a small child on the other end of it. The two of them easily carried the bales over to the spot in the yard Tricia had designated.

Mia paused in her careful unloading of the produce. "How much are they going to be?"

"Oh, right." Tricia had been so focused on getting the inventory out of the fields that she hadn't gotten to that part yet. "I thought I might paint some signs."

The little girl's eyes instantly lit up. "Can I help? I love to paint!"

Once again, Tricia didn't see how she could possibly say no. "Sure. I found some wood scraps in the barn, and we can lay down some cardboard."

While Mason finished unloading, she and Mia rounded up the supplies they would need.

When they returned to the front yard, Oliver was slowly trundling Mia's wagon full of carving pumpkins. "Right down here?" he asked, pointing at a flat spot closer to the road.

That was exactly where Aunt Fiona had always put them, and Tricia hadn't planned to change the tradition. "That would be perfect, thank you. You certainly managed to fit quite a few of them in there."

"There's a lot more, too. I can get the gourds after this." Oliver readjusted his grip on the handle and started toward the spot they'd discussed.

Tricia put a hand out to stop him. "Hold on. What gourds?"

He thumbed over his shoulder. "The ones behind the barn."

"Can you show me what you're talking about?"

With a nod, Oliver dropped the wagon handle. His siblings and Tricia followed him. What she saw behind the barn completely took her breath away. Wire panels had been attached to the top of a small fence and arched over to join another fence. Vines snaked up the sides and threaded through the grids, and beautiful decorative gourds hung down. It was like all of autumn had been summed up into a tunnel.

It was just tall enough for Tricia to step underneath it. She reached up with her good hand and plucked a gourd. "I had no idea this was here. I guess I'd really only gone out into the pumpkin fields, but I hadn't checked to see what was on this side of the barn."

"Isn't it pretty?" Mia said, coming inside and spinning in a circle.

Oliver kicked his shoes in the dusty earth beneath them. "Um, would it be okay to come over here to play sometimes? We used to pretend this was our fort."

"That sounds like just the kind of thing my sister and I would've done when we were younger," Tricia replied wistfully. "Of course you can. You know, I've got some ideas to make this place more than just a plain old pumpkin patch, and you might really like it."

"What are you going to do?" Mia asked. She slipped her hand into Tricia's as they headed back toward the front yard.

She'd already thought they were the most endearing things she'd ever seen when she'd met them at the haunted house, but now she was starting to feel like she'd known these children their whole lives. "Well, I thought it would be fun to have a big painting of a jack-o-lantern with cutouts that you can put your face through and have your picture taken."

Mia hopped on her toes. "Or you could do one with a black cat!"

"I could," Tricia agreed. "You might have to help me paint that one."

"Okay!"

"I want to get in one of those big corn bins," Mason said. "My cousin said he went to a place that had a whole big container full of dried corn, and you could kind of swim around in it."

"Oh. Sort of like a ball pit," Tricia mused. "What about you, Oliver? What would you want to see at a pumpkin patch?"

He seemed to be slightly less outspoken than his younger siblings, and he tipped his head a little as he thought about it. "Hayrides would be nice."

"I thought so, too. Or maybe a bonfire with s'mores." It was clear to Tricia that these kids had just as much hope for the farm as she did. They reached the flattened cardboard box that she'd spread out on the grass, and Tricia handed Mia a paintbrush. "I think we'll start by painting it plain white, and then we can put the numbers on it when it dries."

"There you are!"

All four of them jerked their heads up to see Duke striding through the field, looking angry. Even Tricia felt a twinge in the pit of her stomach as though she were in trouble.

"You were supposed to be out in the backyard," he chided as he joined them. "I looked out the kitchen window, and you were gone."

"I'm sorry, Dad," Oliver volunteered, his fingers still on the handle of the wagon. Tricia could see in the way he moved his fingers over the metal that he hoped he'd get to continue what he was doing. "We just came over to help out Tricia."

"Did you?" Duke's gaze landed on her.

She opened her mouth to reply, but for a moment, nothing came out. It was a good thing she was already kneeling on the ground, or she might have keeled over from that look. Duke had an effect on her, no matter what kind of mood he was in. "I—"

"She was trying to pick the pumpkins," Mason explained before she could get out another syllable. "But she only has one hand, so we came to help. I'm working on the pie pumpkins, and Oliver is getting the big ones. Mia is painting signs."

The chief's eyes flicked over the scene, seeing that all of this was true. His frown straightened out a little. "Be that as it may, you still shouldn't have left the yard without permission. We've talked about that."

"We're sorry," Mia volunteered. "Do we have to come home now?"

Tricia got to her feet, ready to ask him if they could stay. She had no right, and it might just make him angry with her on top of being disappointed, but it was worth the risk. She just didn't want them to leave. She tried to figure out how to explain that they brought this place to life without sounding desperate.

"No," Duke said. "You were right in coming to help someone who needed a hand. Who needed us."

"Really, Daddy?" Mia squealed. "Because I really want to finish painting these signs. Tricia said they're sort of like price tags for the whole place, which means everyone is going to see them. I have to make one for each size."

"And you're doing a very good job of it, too," her father noted.

"I've got the hardest job, getting all the big ones in from the back field." Oliver clearly wanted to be acknowledged for his work just as much as his siblings did. "I've been hauling them all in Mia's wagon. Otherwise, Tricia wouldn't have any way of getting them over here."

"I see that." Duke rubbed his jaw. "You take that wagon over to the pie pumpkins and load both of them up. In the meantime, I'll get the four-wheeler out with the cart I have for firewood, and we can make quicker work of it."

Oliver's eyes lit up. "That's a good idea!"

Duke chuckled softly as he ruffled his son's hair. "I thought so. We'll get it all taken care of."

Tricia smiled to herself as she opened the next can of paint. As soon as she'd come outside, she'd known this day would be a struggle. She'd have to carve a living out of the landscape on her own, even though it would be nearly impossible. Now that she had so many hands helping her, she hardly even knew what to do. "Whoa! I don't think we'll be able to paint the prices on today, Mia. This paint we found in the barn has gotten moldy."

"Let me see!" Mason scrambled over to peer into the big can. "Ugh, that's so nasty! You should see it, Dad!"

Though he'd already taken several steps toward his own place, Duke turned around and obligingly looked in the paint bucket. "Yep. That's definitely moldy. We'll have to dispose of that, but I think I might have some leftovers in the garage that'll work. I'll go look."

Before she knew it, the pumpkin patch was coming together quickly. While she and Mia waited for the base coat of paint to cure, they went down to check the patch of mini pumpkins and make sure they got them all. Mason was an incredibly energetic child, hauling loads of pie pumpkins out of the field all by himself and just as enthusiastically arranging them around the straw bales. Oliver and Duke were just as productive now that they had the four-wheeler's assistance, and the lower part of the yard quickly filled with massive pumpkins destined to be carved and displayed for the holiday.

Sure that the children had to be exhausted, even though they were still working and chattering away, she convinced them to take a break on the porch stairs with peanut butter sandwiches and big glasses of milk. Tricia was just bringing out some sodas for herself and Duke when she paused at the screen door.

"Mia, you really need to eat your sandwich,"

Duke reminded his daughter. "You're going to be hungry later if you don't."

She was busy drawing in the dirt with a stick, her forgotten sandwich in her other hand. "I can't draw a kitty."

Instead of admonishing her to get back to her meal, Duke bent over to look at what she'd drawn. "Sure, you can. You've got one right there."

"But it isn't good enough," Mia protested. "Tricia said I can help her paint a big black kitty cat, the kind you put your face through for pictures. But this one doesn't look very good."

"I think it just needs a tail." He guided the end of her stick in the dirt to add to what she'd already put there. "You can make it curl up around its body, like this."

"Oh, I like that." Mia took a big bite of her sandwich and grinned.

"Hey, Dad. I'm supposed to have a red folder for class tomorrow." Oliver had already downed his sandwich and was nearly done with his milk.

Duke straightened. "A red folder? I don't remember that being on your school supply list."

Oliver shrugged. "I know, but Mrs. Harris said we had to have one for English class to put certain assignments in.   We're supposed to have it by tomorrow."

"And how long have you known about this?" his father asked.

"Um..." The boy rolled his eyes up in his head. "I don't know. Since last week?"

"Make sure you tell me these things as soon as you find out about them so we don't have to rush to the store," Duke replied gently. "That would be a lot easier on all of us."

Oliver nodded. "Okay. Sorry, Dad."

Tricia sighed. The man was incredibly patient. He had to work a lot of long hours, considering his position, and she knew the job wasn't easy. But then he came home and spent time with his children, guiding them carefully and gently. Though she hadn't known him until recently, she could easily guess that he'd always been this way. He wasn't just coddling them because they'd had some tragedy in their lives.

It made her heart reach out toward him all the more, though she tried to snap it back as she pushed the screen door open. Their dinner date had already told them they had no future together, and it wasn't fair to continue torturing herself over it.

"Thank you for everything you've done today,"

she said as she handed Duke the soda. "I can't even tell you how much I appreciate it because I never would've gotten this far on my own."

"We're not done yet," Mason reminded her. "There are still a whole bunch of pumpkins out in the field, and I want to bring all of them in."

"Not without me!" Oliver set his dish aside and shot down the stairs.

"I still have painting to do!" Mia went after them with part of her sandwich still in her hand.

"They're incredible," she said quietly to Duke.

He was proudly watching as his children jumped back to work. "I can't argue with that."

16

It was late. The children, exhausted from their efforts, were safely tucked in their beds. Duke leaned against the back porch railing, smiling to himself as he thought about all they'd done that day. Children were curious, and it wasn't much of a surprise that they'd gone over to see Tricia. After all, they'd already met her, and they knew Duke had shared a dinner with her.

But this had been more than simple curiosity or even friendliness. They'd seen her having a hard time, and they'd left their own agendas behind to go and help her. It'd been more than just a minimal effort, too. Even from there, Duke could see the big rows and piles of pumpkins that'd been assembled in the grass in front of Tricia's house. Mia had finished all the signs, which glowed like ghosts in the moonlight, and she had promised to come back and paint a much bigger one that could be put out on the road to help direct traffic toward the farm.

As soon as he'd understood what they were doing, Duke knew he couldn't make them go home, nor could he go back himself. The three of them were setting a stunning example, and what kind of father would he be if he didn't join in? He'd hesitated for only a moment, knowing that it would be difficult to be so close to Tricia. It would set his bear off all over again as it raged over not claiming her as his.

He'd been wrong, though. As he hauled pumpkins and fetched paint, the beast was content. A sense of peace he hadn't felt since before Tricia arrived—and probably even long before that—had descended over him. Duke had tried to rationalize that working outside did everyone a little good, but he couldn't be fooled. He knew better, but it didn't change anything. Tricia was an independent woman, one who didn't want to be burdened by the baggage he came with.

His eyes roved over to the tree line, seeing nothing but shadows. Others had been watching this border throughout the day and evening. Chris had sent them, and even though there had been no communication about exactly where they were or when they arrived, Duke had known they were there. It was only a small comfort, though. The Johnstons had been quiet. Too quiet. They hadn't shown back up at Tricia's place, nor had they confronted her elsewhere in town. Chris had reached out to Fred Johnston with no reply. There weren't even any factions harassing the logging teams or creating chaos elsewhere in town. Duke would've fully expected that of them if they wanted to create a diversion while they finished taking care of Tricia.

Tricia. Though he knew he shouldn't, Duke let his gaze wander back to her house. She'd left the curtains open. If she were a different person, he might've suspected she'd done it on purpose to lure him over there, to remind him of just what he was missing out on. Tricia wasn't like that, but the reminder was working nevertheless. He'd come out after dinner, and he'd seen her running her free hand through her hair as she waited for something to warm up in the microwave. She'd leaned against the counter while she answered the phone, and later on, she'd grabbed a broom to sweep the kitchen floor. He'd watched her head upstairs, with her bedroom lamp turning off for a while. An hour later, Duke had seen her return.

And that was exactly when he wished he'd watched the border instead of her house. She'd descended the stairs in a cozy robe, the fluffy, over-sized kind that wasn't supposed to be sexy yet somehow was on her. Her hair was piled on top of her head in a clip, still damp from her shower. The glow of light from the refrigerator shone on her face for a moment, and soon enough, she'd returned to the living room and into a chair in front of the fire-place with a big glass of wine. Tricia wiggled her shoulders as she settled into the chair and picked up a book, making the front of her robe gap a little. Even from this distance, he could tell she was wearing nothing underneath it.

His bear perked up, letting go of the last bit of peacefulness he'd found earlier when they were working in the fields together. She had no idea he was watching her, yet she might as well have been trying to entice him. She put her feet up on a nearby stool, raising one knee to brace her book while she wrapped her fingers gently around the stem of her wine glass. The robe fell away to reveal almost the entirety of her leg, sleek and shiny from the attention she'd given it in the shower. Tricia lifted the glass to her lips without taking her eyes off her book.

Duke dug his fingernails into the railing, wishing the tiny splinters from the wood were enough to keep him distracted. But his bear was swelling inside him, reminding him of just how little distance there truly was between them. It wouldn't take much effort to cross his yard and her field, and he could get to her front door with his eyes closed. He'd step across the hardwood floor to her, his hands parting that robe the rest of the way, letting it slide off her shoulders.

His throat had gone dry, and he swallowed. It was a nice fantasy, one that would probably be on his mind for the rest of the night, but he knew it couldn't be. Too many obstacles were in their way. Duke knew he shouldn't even be watching her like this, teasing himself and creating scenes in his head that he could never act out. That night at The Warehouse still lingered in his mind, flaming to life again every time he saw her or even thought about her. He was only making himself suffer, but it was impossible not to zero in on that delectable scene through her living room window. The book would fall from her hand, and the wine would be forgotten on the table. Her hair would tumble down around her, damp and cool against her heated skin.

The sharp shattering of glass exploded into the night. Duke jerked upright, trying to figure out what had happened. Tricia's wine glass was safely on the table next to her, but she was bolting up out of her chair. The book tumbled to the floor, just as he had wanted it to, but not under the same circumstances. She braced her free hand on the arm of the chair as she looked around in alarm, finally grabbing a cast iron poker from the stand on the hearth. Now her glass did fall to the floor, spilling the red liquid onto her robe on the way down.

There it was. Her house was angled just the right way that Duke hadn't been able to get a good view of her back porch, but now he saw the dark figure there. She hadn't turned on the light, but his vision was sharpening as adrenaline rushed through his veins, and his bear threatened to emerge. He could only see one figure there, and he could handle that. Duke hopped over the railing on the back porch, keeping a low profile as he moved swiftly through the grass. If the bastard didn't see him, he couldn't be prepared for the attack that would come from behind.

Duke dared one last glance through the living

room window. The scene in front of the fireplace had been completely disrupted now, and he only caught a glimpse of Tricia's feet as she scrambled upstairs. Good. She'd be out of the way, and he would've taken care of things by the time she was brave enough to come back down.

But as he approached, he realized he wasn't the only figure moving through the darkness. Men streamed out of the woods behind Tricia's house, moving swiftly toward her place. The distance and the dim lighting made it impossible to make them out, but he had no question about their identity. His gut swirled. No wonder the Johnstons had been so quiet lately. They were rounding up their forces, ready to put on a show that would make the Thompsons realize just how serious they were. There were enough of them that they hadn't even bothered to shift yet. At least that meant their senses were no sharper than his own at the moment.

Though it pained him, Duke paused behind the last tree on his property. He keyed in the code Tyler had given him on his cell phone, praying it would work. If he didn't have enough reinforcements, and if they didn't get there on time, everything would be lost. It wouldn't matter how much he loved Tricia. He wouldn't have any reason to curse fate for both bringing them together and pushing them apart because they'd all be dead.

With that done and hope riding on a quick call to arms, Duke raced across the field. The Johnstons were streaming toward her back door now that one of them had managed to pry it open. He veered slightly toward the left, moving toward the front. His police force training had him quickly forming a plan. He knew Tricia was upstairs. He'd keep his human form as long as he could because it would be the easiest way for him to get inside. Then he could catch the onslaught before they could get up to her.

A bear streaked out of the darkness next to him, barreling straight for the enemy. Chase. Another one followed not far behind, emerging from a slightly different angle. Duke was fairly certain it was Evan. Galvanized, he charged on. They weren't at an advantage yet, but at least he wouldn't be doing this alone.

Thundering up the stairs, Duke flung aside the screen door. He hated that he had to keep his human form for the moment, but he needed his hands. His strength as a bear would help, but he only would've gotten tangled up. He twisted the knob and shoved his shoulder into the door. The old wood of the trim sent a loud crack echoing through the covered porch. Another whack had him stumbling into the living room, the splintered wood littering the way.

He could feel her fear inside his bones. It crept into him, making him wonder if any of the others would get there on time. Duke shoved the thoughts aside, knowing they wouldn't do any good. "Stay up there, Tricia!" he called up the stairs.

A roar sounded from the back of the house. A massive bear rushed in from the kitchen, broken glass littering its fur. It didn't seem to mind as it bared its teeth at him, nor was it hampered by the way its wide shoulders slammed into the trim of the narrow doorway. Its claws lost traction for a split second on the area rug Tricia had laid over the threshold between the two rooms, giving Duke just enough time.

It had been desperate to show itself for weeks, but Duke finally called his bear forward. His bones cracked, the sound reverberating inside his skull as his body broke and put itself back together again to accommodate his new shape. Duke's razor-sharp teeth descended from his gums, and his mouth filled with the coppery taste of his own blood. The room around him seemed to shrink as his body grew, his mass too big for a space intended for humans.

His enemy didn't give him the time to finish his shift before it attacked. Its footsteps shook the entire house as it charged, another deep roar issuing from its lungs. The big bear lurched forward, hate and bloodlust in its eyes and saliva dripping from its teeth.

Duke dodged to the side, nearly tripping over the coffee table. He scrambled to keep his footing as he skirted around the giant beast, and his claws sank into the soft cushioning of the sofa. A ripping sound echoed through the air, muffled by the crashing and clanging coming from the kitchen. He could hear his clan members outside, bellowing as they attacked the Johnstons who hadn't yet made it inside the house. Caught between his two forms, Duke made a charge of his own.

17

TRICIA GRIPPED THE POKER AS SHE LOCKED THE bedroom door behind her. Not that it would do a lot of good unless someone got far too close to her. She slipped across the bedroom, hoping to skip the creaky parts of the floor as she crossed to the window.

Her guts curled in on themselves as she saw the intruders coming out of the woods and toward her home. They were just shapes in the moonlight, but the scene was terrifying. It was like an invasion, but she was only one person! How could they possibly all come after her? Was this how far Charlie Johnston was willing to go for a piece of land?

Fear choked her throat as she saw more men

coming out of the woods, but these ones were coming from the east, behind Duke's house. They flew through the night, and her vision seemed to have blurred as she watched. She blinked, trying to regain focus on the scene below, but the men she'd seen were no longer quite men, no matter how hard she tried to look. They were running on all fours, their backs hunching up and their faces stretching into muzzles. It was impossible. She hadn't had that much wine, and she was definitely awake. A gasp escaped her lips as she saw that those coming in from the north were changing as well. It just didn't make sense.

Tricia turned away from the window, feeling sick. She didn't dare try to look again because she couldn't trust whatever she might see out there. Clutching the front of her robe, she tried to figure out what she should do. Call the cops? They'd probably throw her in a padded room if she told them people were turning into bears and attacking her home. Tricia couldn't even expect Duke to believe such a thing. Where had she even left her cell phone? She had to do something. She couldn't just sit there and wait for them to come.

The attic. It was a risk, but maybe she could pull

the ladder up behind her and stay safe for a little while longer until she knew what to do. With her heart in her throat, Tricia cracked open the bedroom door. She could hear something happening downstairs, heavy thumps and crashing. She skittered down the hall, hating to come anywhere closer to the chaos that had taken over her house. Her fingers shook as she reached up for the string on the trap door when a shout rose up the stairs.

Tricia froze. Was that Duke? Could that possibly have been his voice among the other sounds coming up the stairs? And if he were down there, who would save him from the others? Whether they were men, bears, or something in between, she didn't know, but she couldn't just let him die while she hid in the attic.

Readjusting her grip on the poker and knowing she'd never do this if she didn't just dive right in, Tricia ran down the stairs. Her living room was full of brown fur and long claws. Several bears barreled through the front door while another charged in from the kitchen. None of it made sense, but her mind nearly exploded when she looked at the bear near the couch. He had the claws and body of an animal, but his face was changing. She caught a glimpse of it before it was covered completely in fur. For a split second, she swore she saw the deep blue of Duke's eyes.

Another bear attacked him, and she screamed. The others turned to look up at her, their dark eyes alarmed and their noses twitching. One started up the stairs toward her, but another crashed through the railing and took it down. The bear near the couch, who'd looked so much like the man she loved a moment ago, pounced on top of him. She knew that beast down there couldn't possibly be Duke. She wanted to scream again, to call out to them and tell them to stop, to do something to make all of this end.

But the attacker was lifted, snarling and swiping, by the strong, furry arms of the blue-eyed bear. It tossed him straight through the plate glass window above the couch, the same one that faced Duke's house, and the bear tumbled down into the yard. The one who seemed so familiar gave her a look before it shoved its way through the front door and outside. The others loped after him.

Tricia only had to come down one more step to see that the bears were waging a war right in the middle of her pumpkin patch. They trampled the vines and squashed the remaining pumpkins as they gnashed their teeth and swiped their claws. Blood spilled out onto the ground, making dark stains. It was a wild mass of fur as they fought each other, with more jumping in. She couldn't tell who was supposed to be on what side, and she didn't even know what they were fighting for. Tricia watched as more bears came charging into the fight, many coming from somewhere near the road. The battle ensued, with bear after bear dropping to the ground.

The tide had shifted. One bear limped off toward the woods behind her house. Another followed him, and no one pursued them to try to take them down completely. The ones that had invaded her home were leaving, but that still left far too many of these dangerous predators on her territory.

Her eyes drifted down, and she spotted her phone on the coffee table. Tricia knew she might never get another chance to grab it. Keeping an eye on the skirmish outside, she forced her rubbery knees into action once again. The floor was littered with glass and wood that dug into her bare feet. She juggled the poker in her hand as she grabbed her phone and slipped it into the pocket of her robe. One more look through the hole where the window used to be showed her the bear battle had nearly ended. Several beasts lay on the field, blood pouring out of them. Though some were still standing there, ready to fight, others were leaving. Tricia turned back for the stairs.

A bear was standing squarely in her way.

18

TRICIA FELT ODDLY CALM AS SHE WATCHED THE BEAR. She still held the poker in her hand but didn't raise it up to use it. She could have tried heading out the back door, but her feet stayed put.

Blood dampened the bear's chest, running from cuts and scrapes that had been dealt all over his face and shoulders, turning his fur nearly black. One claw had broken, making an odd clicking scrape on the floor as the animal took a step toward her. It lifted its muzzle slightly, and she could see the damp nose twitch as it sniffed the air. Its shoulders relaxed.

At that moment, she understood it wouldn't attack her. That still didn't prepare her for what happened next.

The claws receded into the bear's paws. It let out a small moan, and its body shook as its muscles changed shape. The beast turned its face away from her as its fur retreated back into its skin, but she could still see its ears change position as they moved down the side of its head. The animal was losing mass, no longer nearly as bulky as it'd been only a moment ago, and then it pushed itself up to stand on two feet.

It was no longer a bear. It was Duke.

Her stomach rolled. Tricia's lower lip tucked in, but she couldn't stop the tears that rimmed her eyes. "No."

"Tricia. Are you okay?" Duke stepped toward her. His muscles were tight as though he were ready to go back outside and fight, but the scuffle had ended.

Through the broken window, she could hear the sound of men's voices calling to each other, shouting directions. She didn't even need to look to know that if she turned her head, she'd no longer see bears in the field. "That's not a fair question."

"I know." He moved forward another step, ever so slowly, treating her like she was the wild animal now. "I can explain."

"Really?" How could anyone actually explain

something so deeply unsettling? "I heard you. I heard you call out to me. I came down here, but you weren't here. Not really. So if you think you can explain this, then please do. I want to hear it from your lips."

"It was still me." Those midnight eyes were full of concern. His hair was rumpled. Hair, she realized, that was a similar color to the fur she'd just seen covering his body. His footsteps were slow and calculated as he continued to cross the room toward her. "I didn't *look* like the person you know, but underneath, I was. I'm a shifter. I can change my form when I need to, and right then, I did. I had to stop them."

Her breath was shallow, and her lungs pumped quickly as all the pieces started to fall into place. "It was the Johnstons." She didn't know how, but when she'd seen all those people coming up through the field, she'd been certain.

Duke gave a slight nod. "Yes. There are many shifters around here. Most of us try not to reveal that side of ourselves around humans. It's not the sort of thing people really understand."

"No shit." She almost choked on the words as sobs threatened to overtake her. She turned away from him, not wanting to face him as a tear escaped and trickled down her cheek. Unfortunately, that had her facing the window. She saw now exactly what she imagined she'd see: no bears. It wasn't as though they'd simply walked off, though. They'd changed. "I guess I just..."

"Sit down. I'll get you some water."

"I don't need water," she protested, but she sank onto the sofa. Her hand met stuffing instead of the fabric upholstery, and she looked down to see three huge slashes through the cushion.

"I'm sorry about that," Duke said as he returned with a bottle of water and pressed it into her hand. "In fact, I'm sorry about all of it. I'll make sure I get the window replaced."

A breeze came in through the opening just then, cooling her still-damp hair. "I don't even think I care right now. I just want to understand what the hell happened here."

Duke sat on the couch next to her. He was just far enough away to not be touching her, but he stayed close, perched on the very edge of the cushion. "You know about the feud between the Thompsons and the Johnstons, but you read those letters as though human families were involved. The story behind it is still essentially the same."

She blinked, thrown off by the sudden reference

to such ancient history. "I'm sorry, what the hell does that have to do with tonight? That was forever ago."

"Yes, but like I told you, the two clans—families —have been fighting ever since. We're constantly on alert for what the Johnstons might try to do next because they tend to be rather aggressive. I guess I don't have to tell you that part, though." He sighed as he leaned over and picked a broken lamp up off the floor.

"So I've become part of this feud?" Tricia asked, still trying to wrap her head around it.

"Essentially. This land had been in Johnston hands when your uncle was still alive, but as his wife, Fiona was considered part of the family, so they couldn't do much about it when it went to her. This area is considered the border between the territories belonging to each clan, so it's rather important. Charlie Johnston didn't just want you to sell this to him for sentimental reasons. The more land they own, the more control they have of the area. You showed him that you weren't going to cave and put up with his bullshit, and they decided they'd have to do something drastic to get their way." Duke leaned forward, bracing his elbows on his knees so he could look up into her face.

He was waiting for her to respond, but how could she? "While I guess that helps me understand a little, it really doesn't get to the root of the problem. I would be terrified enough if two rival gangs decided to come fight on my property, but we're not even talking about humans here. You're telling me there's, what, a whole different species that walks around among us?"

His face changed a little, and she could see the hurt there. "Yes. You've probably talked with plenty of us at this point. You most likely even did a shifter's hair back in Eugene. As you just saw, there's no shortage of us."

Tricia closed her eyes, realizing just how big this was. She'd been living among them her entire life, and she hadn't even realized it. "You're one, so I suppose that means your children are, too? I guess they were the three cubs I caught eating my pumpkins a week ago."

He straightened a little, getting that stern dad look on his face. "They aren't supposed to be doing that. I guess they've been sneaking over here more than I thought."

Which explained why the McMillan children seemed to know the farm better than she did, but there was still so much more. Tricia felt the information coming at her like a tsunami as she clutched the cold water bottle in her hand and tried to make sense of everything. "I found a photograph in the attic in the same box I found those letters in. It was an old one of Aunt Fiona, and she was with a bear. That bear was Uncle Dick, wasn't it?"

"I haven't seen the photo, but it's a fair assumption," Duke replied quietly.

"Holy hell." She took a deep drink of the water. "There's more, isn't there? It's not as simple as that. It can't be."

"Yes, but I think that's probably enough for tonight."

Maybe so, and maybe for the rest of her life. "I never should've come out to this fucking place. Maybe I should just pack everything up and go back home to Eugene. I thought I would get a fresh start, but it's been a disaster. It was all a mistake, and I might as well just cut my losses before it gets any worse."

"Would it make any difference if I said I wanted you to stay?" His voice was deep and smooth, but she heard the urgency in it.

Tricia looked around the room. She saw the smashed wine glass on the hearth. Her book lay nearby, the pages creased from falling. Much of the furniture was damaged in some form or another, and deep claw marks scarred the wooden floor. The door stood open, its frame broken and useless.

Anxiety welled up inside her, and she shot to her feet. "I've got to do something about all of this. It's not like I can just go to bed with the door standing wide open. I think I saw some boards and nails out in the barn. Now if I could only find my shoes..." They were usually right there by the door.

"Tricia, you can't go out to the barn in your robe." Duke slowly stood up.

"I can if I want to," she snapped. "It's not like anyone is going to see me, and I'm not sure I care if they do. I just need to get this cleaned up. It's a fucking mess. I'm getting the broom." Tricia stormed past him and into the kitchen.

But she couldn't even cross the floor to get to the broom closet. The linoleum floor was littered with debris, and it took her a moment to realize it had once been her dishes, kitchen table, and chairs. Nothing had been spared as the Johnstons had ransacked her house, pulling out drawers and yanking down shelves. A set of claws had gouged deeply into the front of the old fridge. The back door had been ruined even worse than the front, the couple of boards that remained of it hanging from the hinges.

She gritted her teeth, overwhelmed. There wasn't even a good place to start. "The kitchen was always my least favorite part of this house."

Duke came up behind her. "None of this has to be addressed tonight."

Because she was tired, she thought he was probably right. She was also tired of trying to have any further conversation with him. "Maybe not. I'm going to Tara's."

"I'd rather you didn't." He hooked his hand in her elbow as she tried to get past him once again. "I want to make sure you're safe. I'd like it if you came and stayed at my place."

Their bodies were only a few inches apart, the same position that'd led to their tryst at the Halloween party. She could still feel that deep attraction, even though she knew what lurked inside him. It didn't seem possible, but it was there, and it pissed her off. "How is that going to make me any safer than if I go to Tara's?" she challenged him.

His left hand was still gently gripping her elbow, but he lifted his right to push a tendril of hair out of her face. "Because I've always been here, protecting you. The Thompson clan showed up because I went to our Alpha and explained what Charlie had done to your arm. The fight that happened tonight was me—and everyone else—coming to make sure you were safe. I regret that I couldn't stop it from happening in the first place, but I don't like the idea of you being out in the world without protection. It's... it's kind of a shifter thing."

Tricia hesitated. Duke was asking her to come and stay with him, yet he was the very thing she was having such a hard time understanding. "I don't know."

"There's a guest room right next to mine," he clarified. "You'll have it all to yourself."

She swallowed, unsure if she was more or less tempted now that she knew he wasn't trying to get her into his bed. Tricia glanced to the side, trying to avoid that weighty gaze. She only saw the pure destruction of her house, something she couldn't easily explain to Tara when she hardly understood it herself. "Fine. I'll get my things."

Now in yoga pants and a sweatshirt, she went out onto the porch with Duke just as someone pulled into the driveway. "Great. Now what do I have to deal with?"

"It's all right," Duke said as a burly man with short dark hair got out of the truck. "This is Tyler.

He's going to make sure your house stays safe through the night."

Tricia wanted to know how the hell she was supposed to trust some other random guy who was probably also a bear, but what did she have to lose? It wasn't like her house could get any worse than it already was. "I see."

Tyler nodded to her in greeting before turning to Duke. "Sounds like the system worked. Chris is paying Fred a personal visit right now, or he'd be here, too."

"Good to hear. I'll be at my place if you need anything."

Tricia didn't know what any of it meant. There was clearly so much more going on than could be explained in a few minutes, and she didn't think she could push any more of it into her poor brain right now, anyway. She walked along next to Duke in silence, not saying a word. She followed him into his quiet house, through the shadows of the living room and hallway, until he opened the door into a guest room.

"I know it's going to be difficult," he said quietly, "but try to get some sleep. I'll be right next door if you need anything, and we can talk some more tomorrow."

As she lay awake staring at the ceiling, Tricia realized she'd always known. It wasn't solid knowledge in her brain or a fact she'd read out of a textbook and memorized. It was an intrinsic understanding, something that had seeped inside her at some point. Though she never could've guessed that he was a shifter and could turn into a bear at the drop of a hat, she'd sensed that there was an... *otherness* about him.

Now she knew for sure.

She also knew that he was a man who cared deeply about his children and their wellbeing. He was someone who had enough concern for his community to tackle not only regular street criminals but also whatever threats came from the Johnston clan. Duke had shown her countless times that he was kind, caring, and thoughtful. He'd raised his children to be the same way.

Did that outweigh the fact that he was also a bear? Or was there truly any need to compare the two sides of him?

She couldn't be sure, and she wasn't even sure she'd made the right decision by staying there that night.

19

WHEN THE SUN STREAMED THROUGH THE WINDOW and down onto her face, Tricia realized she hadn't slept in ever since she'd arrived in Carlton. Every day, she'd either been busy organizing her house or trying to figure out how to run a pumpkin farm. Neither one seemed particularly important right now.

She rolled over onto her back, noticing that Duke didn't skimp on sheets, even in the guest bedroom. Much of the terror and tension she'd felt the night before had disappeared into the mattress as she'd gotten the sleep she'd so badly needed. But now what? Her house was a disaster, and the pumpkin patch was completely shot. Any idea of her opening on time to actually have a season was a joke. Tricia hadn't even fully surveyed her land, given that it was still full of man-bears, blood, and moonlight when she'd come through it last night.

What was she going to do now?

Faint shouts and a loud bang filtered into the room. Tricia listened, hearing what sounded like a diesel truck. What the hell was happening? She sat up and swung her legs out of bed. Whatever it was, she was going to face it head-on.

Following the scent of coffee and bacon, she found an older woman sitting peacefully at the kitchen table. She looked up from her newspaper and smiled. "Good morning, sunshine. I thought you might sleep right through to lunch, but I saved you some breakfast. I'm Emily, by the way. I'm the nanny."

Wondering just how much Duke had or hadn't told her, Tricia didn't know if she ought to be embarrassed or not. "That's very kind of you. I think I might just take a little for the road if that's all right. I've got some things to take care of today."

Emily gave her a curious look, but she nodded. "Sure. There are some paper plates right here. You can take a travel mug from that cabinet. Duke won't mind."

There had been no other mention of Duke nor

any sign of him. She didn't see the children, either, which kept her from having to explain why she'd been there the night before. Tricia raked her fingers through her hair and stepped out onto the front porch.

The sight that greeted her as she looked over at her place was astonishing. People swarmed the place like ants, and the driveway was packed with vehicles. A large delivery truck had backed up to the porch, where she saw Tyler and another man unloading a new front door. The last of the pumpkins were being brought in from the field, and someone was cleaning up all the vines that'd been broken. A small dumpster had been parked over in front of the barn, and it held the remains of her kitchen table and cabinets. Tricia slowly walked through the field, wondering if she was dreaming.

"Tricia! Daddy, it's Tricia!" Mia came bursting through the yard toward her, paint covering her little hands. "You weren't supposed to be awake yet!"

"I'm not sure that I am," she murmured, putting her hand on Mia's back as the girl wrapped her arms around Tricia's legs. "What's going on here?"

"Look, I painted another sign!" Mia gestured happily to a large piece of fabric being pinned up onto a food cart. The sheet served as a new sign, which read 'Pies!' in a child's handwriting.

Tricia obviously didn't quite know what Mia meant, but she didn't want to extinguish the girl's enthusiasm. "That's very nice, honey."

Mason joined them now, and he tugged on the hem of her shirt in his excitement. "Did you see the corn bin? I mean, it's just a trough right now, but the farmer down the road is coming back to fill it with dried corn. Then we're going to swim in it!"

"She doesn't care about that," Oliver said as he set a big pot of mums down next to several others. "Girls like flowers, and now we've got plenty of them."

"Tricia." Duke came jogging down off the porch. "I hope we didn't wake you up with the noise."

"It's not really the noise I'm concerned about," she tried to explain. There was so much going on that it was hard to know where to look. "What's going on here?"

"This is our clan, and we're here to help. We've got two new doors and a new window being put in. Several ladies have gone inside to clean up, and we've got about everything out to the dumpster. Amy got Lenora Millhouse to volunteer an old food cart that someone had abandoned on her property, which is being converted into a pie wagon. We've got some more items coming, too, but everything should be put back to rights before you know it." He said it so simply, as though this were an everyday thing.

"Kids, could you excuse us for just a moment, please?" Tricia waited until the children had left them before she turned a hard eye on Duke. "You don't have to do this. I don't want your pity."

"It's not pity. It's what we do." Duke stepped closer, resting his hands on her arms. "Tricia, I know you've gone through a lot lately, and I can't expect you to understand or accept everything right away. But for better or worse, the two of us are meant to be together. You're just as much a part of the clan as I am at this point, and we take care of our own."

She opened her mouth to argue, but how could she? What she saw around her was everything she wanted to do with the pumpkin patch but didn't have the time or strength to achieve. These people, practically strangers, were pulling together her vision when they could just as easily have left her with a destroyed home and a ruined business.

And then there was Duke. It was hard to look at him and not see the wild beast he'd become the night before. Everyone had secrets, though, and that part of him hadn't changed who he truly was. Tricia would have said she didn't believe in fate if anyone had asked her. Until now.

"All right," she finally conceded. "But only if you let me help."

He looked doubtfully down at her arm.

"You can't stop me any more than I can stop you. I still have one good hand, after all." She held up her right arm and wiggled her fingers.

"Fine. Then you're with me. There's still plenty of work to be done."

Tricia had doubts and thought she'd be much better off working alone or even with a random stranger. She still felt some of that tension between them that'd built up in her living room the night before as she'd tried to come to terms with it all. They tied scarecrows to the front porch railing, and his fingers brushed against hers. Their eyes met as they decided exactly where the photo props the children had painted should go. Inside the house, she noticed that he didn't stray more than a few inches from her as they surveyed the damage, and he discussed what still needed to be done. Every time Duke introduced her to someone— and there were plenty of people to be introduced to— the clan member regarded her with a knowing smile.

Did they all know something she didn't? Tricia was starting to think she *did* know. Just as she'd known that Duke wasn't like any other guy that she'd ever been interested in. They sensed what was between them, even though she'd refused to see it herself for the longest time.

Her phone buzzed with a text from Tara. *Hey! I've been busy with the winery but wanted to check in. How's everything going?*

How could she possibly begin to explain everything that'd happened over the last twenty-four hours without sounding like a complete nutbag? *Oh, I'm just hanging out with Duke ;) His friends are helping me fix up the place. I'll stop by the winery over the weekend and we can catch up.*

Okay! Tara replied. *I want to hear all the details!*

Over the last forty-four years, they'd told each other everything. But as she tucked her phone back into her pocket, in her heart, Tricia knew this clan's secret wasn't hers to share.

"Dad!" Oliver shouted several hours later as the crowd was finally starting to disperse. "Emma, Liam, and Kinsley said we could come over to have dinner and play tonight. Can we go? Please?" He and his siblings were bouncing with excitement despite all the energy they'd put into the pumpkin patch that day.

"Sure. I think you deserve it. Not too late, though, okay?"

"Okay!" The children ran off to join the others, waving goodbye. They climbed into a big black SUV with several other kids, and the last of the cars headed out toward the road.

"What do you think?" Duke stood next to her on the porch. He spoke of all that'd been done around them, but his eyes were on her.

Tricia smiled as she turned away from him and looked out into the yard, which seemed almost too quiet after all that activity. The Thompson clan had done remarkable work, making it almost impossible to tell that a brawl between two rival bear factions had happened there less than twenty-four hours ago. The sun slowly sank, casting its golden light through the turning leaves and across the beautifully arranged pumpkin patch. It was the textbook definition of autumn.

There had been more people on her property that day than she could count, but she was really only interested in one of them. Tricia had seen the way he'd put so much of himself into the work that needed to be done, not just completing tasks but making sure they were done right. That was exactly who he'd proven himself to be over and over, whether he had a bear inside him or not. There was still a lot she didn't understand, but she was beginning to understand the most important parts.

"It's beautiful, and I can't tell you or the others just how much I appreciate it. But one more thing still needs to be taken care of."

Duke's forehead creased. "I know the kitchen still needs a lot of work, but Pax said he'd come back and go over some design ideas with you. He's kind of a snob when it comes to cabinetry and woodwork, and he didn't want to just slap up some store-bought units."

Tricia laughed as she opened the screen door and stepped inside. "It's not that."

He followed her as she headed up the stairs. "I thought all the damage happened down here."

She continued up the stairs, aware of how it felt to have him in her home. It wasn't the first time, but it all felt different now. That connection she'd experienced had deepened in an unexpected way, one that made her feel as though she were tuned in to every footstep, every breath.

When she reached her bedroom door, she

turned around to look at him. "I think there's still a little work to do in here."

"Yes." His voice was husky as he put his hands on her hips. "I can see that."

Their lips met. Tricia had wondered if it would feel strange to do this again now that she knew exactly who and what he was. But that truth between them had the opposite effect. The very air she breathed was infused with him as she allowed her hands to roam up his chest and across his shoulders. The torture that she'd felt for weeks as she'd wrestled with her feelings for him dissipated now that she was in his arms again.

"You know," he murmured as he tilted his head to nibble on her ear, "it's still not fair that you've gotten to see me naked, and I haven't had the same privilege."

She laughed as she found the hem of his shirt and lifted it over his head with one hand. Tossing it aside, Tricia smoothed her fingers through the dusting of chest hair. "That doesn't count."

"No?" Duke easily released the buttons on the front of her shirt. Careful not to bump her cast, he swept the fabric to the floor.

Tricia closed her eyes as he dipped his head to

drop kisses between her breasts. She ran her fingers through his hair. "Definitely not."

He pressed his hands against her lower back to pull her closer as he returned his attention to her lips. "Why is that?"

She thrilled at the way his voice reverberated against her mouth. "Because I couldn't touch you then."

With a deep growl that managed to bring her simmering passion to a rolling boil, Duke stripped her of her yoga pants. Her fingers acted quickly to remove the final barrier between them, shoving aside his jeans and boxer briefs.

Duke wrapped his arms underneath her and easily carried her to the bed. "You can touch me now."

"I plan to." Tricia stretched out alongside him. He was just as sexy as he'd been that first time she'd spotted him through the window, but knowing he was looking back at her made the view infinitely better. They came together, touching, caressing, exploring. Every movement of his body against hers sent a thrill through her.

Pushing him back against the pillow, Tricia straddled his hips. She leaned forward to kiss him, feeling her body already start to coil inside as his shaft slid against her. Duke put his hands on her ribs to keep her from putting any weight on her broken arm, his thumbs stretching inward to caress her breasts.

She could spend time with him like this forever, but her body and soul craved more. Tricia sank down on top of him, feeling relief as he filled her completely. The reality was just as exquisite as the fantasy of him, and the torment of staying away from him melted into rapture. Their bodies moved together, syncing effortlessly.

Her fervor continued to build, and she knew that Duke was feeding off of it. His nails scraped gently on her skin, and his girth expanded inside her. Tricia sucked in her breath as she luxuriated in the knowledge of their mutual desire. A trembling sigh slipped from her lips as the tightly wound spring he'd created within her finally released, and Duke gripped her hips and joined her. Exhausted, she fell alongside him, and he turned to wrap her in his embrace.

So many times in her life, she hadn't been certain about her future. In this moment, her time with Duke stretched into all of eternity. She wanted to look back and laugh at herself for fighting so hard against something so beautiful.

20

"OH, MY! WHAT WONDERFUL COSTUMES! SOME FOR the ringmaster, some for the ballerina, and some for the cowboy!" The old woman reached into the big bucket she held in her arms and dumped a generous handful of candy into each of the kids' bags.

"What do you say?" Tricia prompted.

"Thank you!" they rang out in chorus before they came charging back down the sidewalk where Duke and Tricia were waiting.

Duke peered inside their bags. "Looks like you guys are getting pretty full."

"Aw, does that mean we have to be done?" Mia asked, trailing her hand through her tutu.

"No way," Tricia answered. "We still have

another neighborhood, and I have extra bags in the car."

"How did you know to do that?" Duke asked as he watched her help the children empty their full treat bags into the much larger bags she'd stashed in the trunk.

She gave him a look. "I was a kid once, too, you know. My mom started doing this after I dropped my bag on someone's porch, and most of it went down between their deck boards, never to be seen again. The older we got and the more time we spent out trick-or-treating, the more it made sense to dump our haul every now and then."

"Sweet!" Oliver jiggled his empty bag in his hand. "Now we can go over there?"

Duke nodded. "Looks like we can."

"Hold hands before we cross the street," Tricia reminded them as they turned for the curb.

With all five of them linked through their hands, Duke couldn't remember ever having a better Halloween. Happiness radiated through him as they went up one side of Carlton and down the other, hitting every house and business with their lights on. Duke saw the same peace in his children's eyes that he felt in himself, and he didn't let go of Tricia's hand even when they were safely on the opposite sidewalk.

The kids started up the next row of houses, their bags once again filling with candy. The sidewalks were crawling with every cartoon character, super-hero, and movie villain that had ever existed, but the children always seemed to recognize their friends despite the masks and makeup.

"There you go!" said a young couple who had both crowded into their doorway along with their dog, thrilled at all the trick-or-treaters. "Your costumes are awesome!"

"Thank you!" Mia called, turning to look over her shoulder as she navigated the last step. Her ankle rolled and she flew forward, sending Smarties and lollipops sprawling over the sidewalk.

"Oh!" Tricia immediately dropped Duke's hand and rushed forward, picking Mia up to assess the damage. "Where does it hurt?"

Mia was crying too hard to answer, and Tricia pulled her in on her shoulder without concern for the snot and tears that would inevitably get smeared on her shirt. "It's okay, sweetie. We'll get you all cleaned up."

The young couple had rushed out, horrified, while their dog anxiously watched through the storm door. "Is she all right? I think we might have some bandages or something."

Tricia smiled at them and waved off their concerns. "Thank you, but we'll be okay."

The boys had picked up Mia's candy for her, and Tricia carried her out to the sidewalk. "Back to the car. I've got a first aid kit in there."

Duke knew that Tricia was something else, but he couldn't help but be impressed at this. "You really did think of everything."

"I did my best, but let's not test it." She stroked her hand through Mia's hair as Duke opened the back hatch of the station wagon, which served as a perfect seating area for small children.

Mia had calmed down somewhat, but big tears still dripped down her face as she watched Tricia clean up the scrape on her palm. "Does *this* mean we have to stop trick-or-treating?" she whimpered.

"I don't think so," Tricia replied. "Not as long as you're still up for it. I've just got to get a bandage on your knee."

Looking down, Mia's tears started over again in earnest. "I ripped my tights!"

"Oh, baby." Tricia kissed her forehead. "That's all right. We can get another pair."

"But now I won't be a pretty ballerina anymore!" Mia wailed.

Duke was just about to volunteer to run to the store when Tricia had a better solution. "That just means you're a zombie ballerina instead! A scary one that will dance fear right into the hearts of other trick-or-treaters! Muahahahaha!"

A hiccupping laugh made its way through Mia's tears. "Ballerinas aren't scary."

"They can be," Tricia countered.

Still uncertain, Mia looked down at her knee. "But it's just a Band-Aid. I don't really look like a zombie."

"Okay. Hang on." Tricia pulled a small makeup bag out of her purse. She swept dark shadow all around Mia's eyes and just below her cheekbones. With a tiny black pencil, she drew a line of stitches on her forehead. With an expert hand, she pulled several tendrils of hair out of the carefully coifed bun that she'd put in Mia's hair earlier that afternoon. Then she pulled out a mirrored compact to show Mia her work. "How's that?"

Mia's eyes widened. "Wow! Yeah!"

"I want to be a zombie!" Mason said. "Can you do me?"

"Make me look like my head fell off and got stitched back on again!" Oliver begged.

It didn't take long for her to do as they asked, and soon enough, they were going back out for more candy. Mia didn't have any further complaints about her ripped tights. The next house had a huge yard that the owners had turned into a makeshift haunted house, and several of the kids' friends happened to be there as well.

Knowing they had at least a few minutes to themselves, Duke took her hand once again. "That was impressive. I knew you were a hairdresser, but I didn't know you were a makeup artist as well."

She shrugged, but she was smiling proudly as she watched the twins talk to their friends. "I guess we all have our secrets."

His heart warmed toward her all over again. Tricia liked to make little jabs at him about his bear, but it was always in a way that let him know she had accepted it. She'd even asked him if she should go as Goldilocks and the children could be the three bears. "It's kind of funny, you know."

"What's that?" She turned to him, her gaze soft.

If he wasn't the chief of police, and if they didn't have dozens of parents and kids there as witnesses, he would've taken her into his arms and shown her everything he felt. At the moment, though, he could only tell her. "I remember you saying something about not wanting kids, but anyone would be hard pressed to know that Mia, Mason, and Oliver weren't yours."

"I did say that," she said with an affirming nod. "Because I don't want just any kids. I want *these* kids. And I want you."

He kissed her, but he was limited to a quick peck as the kids came running back. They finished up the neighborhood, and then it was time to go home.

"Did everyone have a good Halloween?" Tricia asked as they all packed into the car.

The shouts of enthusiasm from the back were enough to let her know the answer, even if they were too excited to sound like any actual words.

"What about you?" Duke asked, firing up the engine. "You've sold all your pumpkins, and the farm is closed for the season. What are you going to do until it's time to plant in the spring?"

"Plenty," she said as she glanced with a smile into the backseat. "But I also talked to Tara about that. She needs some help, and I'll spend some time working over at Cloud Ridge."

"Sounds like a plan to me, as long as it makes

you happy." He laced his fingers through hers and lifted her hand to his lips, kissing the back of it.

"There's a lot that makes me happy right now."

Back at the house, the kids struggled out of their costumes and washed their faces. Tricia disappeared into the kitchen, and Duke found one of their favorite Halloween movies streaming. Everyone piled into the living room, where Duke and Tricia went through the massive load of candy the kids had hauled in before they settled down in front of the TV.

It wasn't always easy to get time alone together. Their lives were full with their jobs and the children, and there were always chores to be done or errands to run. As much as Duke loved the times when they could sneak up to bed early or sleep in a little, he was just as satisfied to cuddle up on the couch next to Tricia while the kids piled around them. He found that he wasn't even paying attention to the movie, concentrating more on the way it felt to be this close to her. Both his bear and his human side felt the deep satisfaction he had at not only being with her, but in knowing that all of them were together. This was his family. This was exactly what he thought he'd never be able to have again.

She turned to him slowly when she realized he was staring at her. "What?" she asked with a smile.

He leaned close so that he spoke only in her ear. "Does all of this mean you believe me? That you know just as well as I do that we're fated?" Duke had only had the chance to glaze over the idea when he'd first told her, but they'd had a lot of long talks since then. He knew that Tricia had held plenty of doubts at first, and he couldn't blame her. He'd certainly had his own, but the more time they spent together, the more sure he was.

Tricia was his mate, the other half of his soul, and he couldn't imagine a life without her.

She pressed her lips together as she surveyed the living room. Mia was curled up at her side, still wearing her tutu over her pajamas. Oliver had sprawled out on the floor, stacking his candy into various piles by type. Mason was stretched backward over the ottoman, watching the movie upside down. She turned her gaze finally to Duke and snuggled deeper under his arm. "If this is my destiny, then I'm more than willing to accept it."

He pressed his lips to hers, feeling that connection between them become even stronger. That was how it was every day for him, and he had no doubt it would continue. Not a moment passed that he didn't fall more in love with Tricia, and he saw that love reflected in her eyes. Duke had never imagined that he could be this happy again.

THE END

If you enjoyed *Next Door Midlife Bear*, you'll love *Bear's Midlife Christmas*! Read on for a preview of Corey and Tara's story.

COREY

"Don't look so sad now that it's finally time to close," Tricia said as she locked the entrance to Cloud Ridge Winery. "I think just about everyone in Carlton has come through those doors."

"I just hope I did everything right, you know? I've got a lot riding on this open house. I don't want to blow my chance to make a good first impression on everyone in the area." Tara Fitzpatrick-Day looked around the room. It was still early in December, but she'd already decorated every surface for the holidays. The sleek, modern winery boasted an elegant Christmas tree in the front window, and gold garland had been draped over the mantel and framed paintings on the walls. Electric candles flickered, enhancing the cozy atmosphere.

"It was fine," Shannon assured her, tucking a strand of her dark hair behind her ear. "More than fine, actually. You had a great turnout, and I'm pretty sure everyone took one of those coupons on their way out. You'll be flooded with holiday business over the next couple of weeks."

"You'll definitely have to keep this new wine in stock, though," Michelle said as she wagged an empty bottle in the air. "I'll have to pretend I don't know about it. I only have so much time to get out and have a few glasses with a baby at home, and it's damn good stuff!"

"You ladies are too kind." Tara didn't know how her twin sister Tricia had managed to make so many friends since their impromptu move to Carlton, but she'd found quite the collective of fun women. "I just inherited this place from my aunt, and I feel like I'm still winging it. I know there's a lot of competition around here, so I want everything to be perfect."

"You *always* do," Tricia chided. "You're doing great. The winery looks beautiful for the holidays, and the wine itself is incredible."

"She's right," Jenna agreed. "If this weren't such a classy place, I'd tell you to market it as being better than sex."

"It's way better than my first time, anyway,"

Shannon snickered. "I was dating this jock who'd built himself up as this experienced guy who knew all sorts of things about how to please a woman. I'm ashamed to say I was dumb enough to believe him. It ended in about five seconds."

"I don't know," Michelle replied with a smirk. "That might be better than a guy who tries too hard."

Tricia refilled her glass from the bottle on the table. "Oh no. What did he do?"

"More like what *didn't* he do," Michelle quipped. "I swear he was trying to recreate one of the movies he used to steal from his dad's sock drawer. He had me all twisted up like a freaking pretzel! It took me a while to figure out why anyone even bothered doing it after that experience."

"I hear you." Jenna drained the last sip from her glass and set it down. "I remember all my girlfriends in high school talking about hooking up with their boyfriends and how great it was, so I thought I was missing out. Of course, my boyfriend was thrilled that I'd finally changed my mind. I just wish his grandmother hadn't walked in on us. We were both traumatized."

The women were laughing so hard now that Tara

could barely hold onto her wine glass. She swiped a tear away from her eye.

"What about you?" Shannon asked. "Did you have to suffer as badly as we did?"

"No, not exactly." Tara studied the way the flames reflected in her glass as she turned the stem in her hands.

"Oh, boy." Her twin gently elbowed her. "Here comes the Corey Story."

"Ooo, sounds like a good one," Shannon said with a smile.

"You know, it really was," Tara admitted. "It was over spring break during my senior year of high school. Tricia and I had come up here to Carlton to visit our aunt, which we tried to do a few times a year. I knew I'd be going off to college, so it would be harder to come up and see her as often, and I really wanted to spend some time with her. But I had to make up for that later because I ended up spending all my time with a boy I met."

"And left me sitting around bored off my ass the whole time," Tricia added. "Then when she came back to the farm, it was all, 'Corey's so funny. Corey's so hot. He's the most amazing guy I've ever met. I think I'm in *love*.' Ugh. It was gross."

"You were just jealous," Tara teased, even though

she knew that wasn't really the case. The girls had spent plenty of time talking about that week in the months and years afterward. "It was pure kismet when we met, like we were meant to be together. I'm sure I was super annoying going on and on about him, but I couldn't help it. He was my first, and he was so sweet and gentle. We promised to call each other and try to do the long-distance thing because what we had was special. But then I never heard from him again. Even when I paged him with our special code, I got nothing."

"Typical guy, and we always fall for it," Shannon said.

"Oh my god," Michelle giggled. "I almost forgot about beepers! My friends and I never left the house without ours back in the nineties."

"Same here," Shannon agreed. "There should be a class that teaches girls everything guys say to try to get into your pants. 'I love you. I'm not like other guys. You're the only girl who's made me feel this way.' I've talked with my daughter about it a lot, but I think plenty of her friends have fallen victim to that sort of thing."

Maybe it was just the wine making her feel all cozy inside, or perhaps because it was easier to reflect on things that'd happened twenty-six years ago, but Tara wasn't convinced any of that had been the case with Corey. When he'd looked into her eyes and told her how much she'd meant to him, she'd known he was telling her the truth. She'd often wondered what would've happened between them if they'd had a chance to be together for more than just that one week.

"Speaking of men, it looks like some of ours are here to pick us up," Michelle said as she glanced out into the parking lot.

A big smile came over Tricia's face. "I told Duke he didn't have to come tonight, but he insisted. He's so sweet."

"Now who's being disgusting?" Tara taunted as she poked her sister in the ribs. "You're all mushy inside."

Tricia swiped her hand away and laughed. "And I *love* it."

"He seems really good for you," Tara said as the two of them got up and went to the doors to unlock them. "I don't think I've ever seen you this happy."

"You definitely haven't," Tricia agreed. "He's the best, and you know how long it took me to find anyone who was even worth a second date. I tried to resist him at first, but I just couldn't."

"I wonder if I'll ever have that again," Tara

mused as they waited for the men to walk up from the parking lot. "I mean, I thought I did with Clint before life and kids got in the way. Not that I'm looking, but... you know."

"I do." Tricia touched her arm. "And you will. I think we all just have to wait for the right time, even though that's the hardest thing to do."

"Hey, honey." Duke came through the door, bringing a bold breeze in with him. The chief of police pressed his lips to Tricia's before giving her a warm look. "I missed you."

"It's only been a few hours," she reminded him.

He shrugged. "Doesn't matter. You know my coworker, Landon. Landon, this is Tara, Tricia's sister."

"I can tell." Landon shook Tara's hand and paused. "Have we met before?"

They shared a glimmer of recognition. *Landon.* Tara's spine stiffened. She'd heard plenty about him through Michelle, but she hadn't made the connection. "Yeah, I think we have."

"This is my brother, Corey. Corey, you might remember Tara, and this is her sister, Tricia." Landon stepped aside to reveal a third man lingering in his shadow.

When he stepped into the light, Tara's heart

froze. Everyone else was still talking around her as they got up and found their jackets, but she only heard it as buzzing in her ears. He was older now, his dark hair having turned salt-and-pepper, but there was no mistaking those eyes. A deep brown like the darkest earth, with a thick fringe of lashes that was still several shades darker than his natural hair color. They were wide eyes, the eyes of a boy that turned down slightly at the corners, and the same eyes she'd looked into all those years ago. "Corey."

————

ALSO BY MEG RIPLEY

ALL AVAILABLE ON AMAZON

Shifter Nation Universe

Fated Over Forty Series

Wild Frontier Shifters Series

Special Ops Shifters: L.A. Force Series

Special Ops Shifters: Dallas Force Series

Special Ops Shifters Series (original D.C. Force)

Werebears of Acadia Series

Werebears of the Everglades Series

Werebears of Glacier Bay Series

Werebears of Big Bend Series

Dragons of Charok Universe

Daddy Dragon Guardians Series

Shifters Between Worlds Series

Dragon Mates: The Complete Dragons of Charok
Universe Collection (Includes Daddy Dragon Guardians
and Shifters Between Worlds)

More Shifter Romance Series

Beverly Hills Dragons Series

Dragons of Sin City Series

Dragons of the Darkblood Secret Society Series

Packs of the Pacific Northwest Series

Compilations

Forever Fated Mates Collection

Shifter Daddies Collection

Early Novellas

Mated By The Dragon Boss

Claimed By The Werebears of Green Tree

Bearer of Secrets

Rogue Wolf

ABOUT THE AUTHOR

Steamy shifter romance author Meg Ripley is a Seattle native who's relocated to New England. She can often be found whipping up her next tale curled up in a local coffee house with a cappuccino and her laptop.

Download *Alpha's Midlife Baby,* the steamy prequel to Meg's Fated Over Forty series, when you sign up for the Meg Ripley Insiders newsletter!

Sign up by visiting www.authormegripley.com

Connect with Meg

amazon.com/Meg-Ripley/e/B00Z8I9AXW
tiktok.com/@authormegripley
facebook.com/authormegripley
instagram.com/megripleybooks
bookbub.com/authors/meg-ripley
goodreads.com/megripley
pinterest.com/authormegripley

Printed in Great Britain
by Amazon

21451539R00150